NIGHT MOVES

NIGHT MOVES

STORIES

RICHARD VAN CAMP

Enfield & Wizenty
(an imprint of Great Plains Publications)
233 Garfield Street
Winnipeg, MB R3G 2M1
www.greatplains.mb.ca

Great Plains Publications gratefully acknowledges the financial support provided for its publishing program by the Government of Canada through the Canada Book Fund; the Canada Council for the Arts; the Province of Manitoba through the Book Publishing Tax Credit and the Book Publisher Marketing Assistance Program; and the Manitoba Arts Council.

Design & Typography by Relish New Brand Experience
Printed in Canada by Friesens

LIBRARY AND ARCHIVES CANADA CATALOGUING IN PUBLICATION

Van Camp, Richard, 1971-, author
    Night moves / Richard Van Camp.

Short stories.
Issued in print and electronic formats.

ISBN 978-1-927855-23-2 (paperback).--ISBN 978-1-927855-24-9 (epub).--
ISBN 978-1-927855-25-6 (mobi)

    1. Title.

PS8593.A5376N44 2015   C813'.54   C2015-903702-6
                                          C2015-903703-4

ENVIRONMENTAL BENEFITS STATEMENT

Great Plains Publications saved the following resources by printing the pages of this book on chlorine free paper made with 100% post-consumer waste.

TREES	WATER	ENERGY	SOLID WASTE	GREENHOUSE GASES
14	6,731	7	451	1,241
FULLY GROWN	GALLONS	MILLION BTUs	POUNDS	POUNDS

Environmental impact estimates were made using the Environmental Paper Network Paper Calculator32. For more information visit www.papercalculator.org.

Canadä

FSC
www.fsc.org
MIX
Paper from
responsible sources
FSC™ C016245

For Keavy and Edzazii: my everything...

bornagirl

Steve nods as Dougie lifts me off the ground. I smell scalp, tar, heat. Pelicans soar miles above us. *That's me, I think. That's who I used to be.* I huff, puff and push all my air out. I wish the sky would blow me in half as Dougie squeezes my ribs tight—so tight my face burns and balloons. I see three pelicans soaring above and wonder if they can see me back and—*Why?*

Heat from my skull explodes and *there they are:* sparks of day fire. Dougie bear hugs me and holds me high—I hear a rib pop—and the next thing I know my ears are roarin' and I rise from the whoosh, and I have a two-by-four. I'm all chased out as my head roars as everyone cheers, "Zombie!"

I see all the grade eights and nines flee, spilling over the fence and road in terror against me. Clarence has climbed to the top of a tree and Dougie is crying, holding his leg going, "Fuck you, Ronny!" and I drop the two-by-four and collapse sore-throated and body ringing. My body spills of everything. *Why? Why did we do it? Why did I do it?*

After, Steve drags me, holds me, walks me home and grins, "That was the best Zombie yet."

My eyes puff out of their sockets and everybody looks so much younger with short hair, even the teachers, even the principal and now the mayor and the chief of the Salt River

First Nations and the president of the Métis Association and now the chief of the Fitz Smith Band and now our MLA, and we are waiting to hear about our MP, but his wife—I know for sure his wife cut hers. What happened here was on CBC and it's spreading. Everyone's cut their hair because of what happened to Brian. And what we did to him. What I did to him. My face goes numb when I think about it, so I don't.

We listen to Stars' "Winter Bones" in the dark, and Steve lies behind me, and I wonder if we're fags. I don't care. I think I'm dying faster than everybody because of Zombie. I accept it. Steve's a chronic shoplifter from the drugstore and today his underarms smell like mint. He reaches over me for a sip of water. "What do you think about?"

I shift my body closer as the mattress sinks. "When?"

I'm blushing with how close we are. I can also smell the detergent his mom uses: Lemon something.

"When you're out," he says. "When you're a zombie. Where do you go?"

"I don't know." He brushes my hip as he shifts, but I know. I think I know. I think of the girl who does Brian's makeup in the handicapped washroom. Kelsey. The redhead. Pretty, blue-eyed and Mayday princess Kelsey. She must know we can all see her glow-in-the-dark scars on her wrists. How she must wince when the shower hits. I remember her when we were in kindergarten, how she used to stand alone under the fort and shiver, even when it was hot out. I'm going to try and tell her to stop being so scared of herself the next time I see her. I want to do that. I hope I remember to do that.

Or I could fuck her for practice.

I also think about beating up Brian. I loved making him cry. I'd race after him when I saw him. "Makeup Warrior," I called him, and then I'd ask, "Why?" (punch) "Why?" (shove) "Why?" (kick) "Why?" (knee). I'd Sally Cow him so he couldn't use his arms and then Charlie Horse him so he'd push to the ground. "You fuckin' fag. Why?" He'd start to cry and I'd grin. I kept trying to knock him out with a punch to the temple or a knee to the chin but he'd tuck his head away. *Why?*

I feel Steve's breath against the back of my neck. I am the most dangerous zombie in Fort Smith history even though this town is the illusion of life. We Zombie every chance we get. Sometimes we use hockey socks or bandanas by ourselves, but mostly we just huff each other, and this is why I'm dying faster than anyone.

I feel like I'm running out of skin.

I can tell Dougie totally fakes when it's his turn to Zombie, and Steve just sits there drooling through his hands. Nobody but me lifts the two-by-four to chase the crowd. The students wait for me to do it, and the teachers never catch on because they're all smoking off school property and texting their old ladies now that Smith got cellphones.

Sometimes, when Steve holds me in the dark, he'll reach for a sip of water or to fiddle with the remote, but it's only really to buck into me slowly. I bet if we were ever naked he'd go for it and maybe I'd let him. We never talk about this, but we do it every time now after Zombie.

Our town is Fort Smith, NWT. Métis capital of the north. Our dance hall is the Roaring Rapids Hall but it's also known as Moccasin Square Gardens because of all the fights. They say Fort Smith is home to the rough and ruthless and the tough and toothless. I've tried to figure out why we Zombie, and I know it's about being held. I lean into Steve. I love it when he holds me. My body sings with his muscles and the smell of his hot scalp and dad's cologne: a quiet fire, something pretty, something burning. I sniff it every time we're over at his house in the bathroom watching pornos.

"Why?" I yelled at Brian as mascara ran down his face. "Why do you dress like a girl when you're a boy? Why?" I loved how his body twisted and gave under my punches. I'd drive his body with each upper cut, and I loved the sounds he made as he slumped into me. He was wearing a skirt and heels. "Why? Why the fuck are you like this?"

But this is not the worst I've done to him.

Last night, me and Steve were walking by the college. I flushed the toilet downstairs and snuck out while the sound was loud and there was Steve with his bike and mine. He knows my combo. We rode out together and the town was ours.

We rode up to the Welfare Centre and to Frontier Village and even to both trailer courts and then by the college residences.

There, we passed by a volleyball team. Girls. Diamond Jenness hoodies. Hay River girls.

"Heyyyyyyyyyy," one with huge glasses on said as we drove by.

Steve hit the brakes. "Helloooooooooooo."

I wanted to keep going but they surrounded us.

"Got a mickey?" one of them asked.

"No," Steve said.

"Well, we do." Big Glasses said and the rest laughed. "Wanna party with us?"

"Sure," Steve said. He gave me a look like we'd struck gold. I wanted to go home.

Before I knew it, we stashed our bikes and snuck in through the ground floor windows at the college residence.

"Shhh," Big Glasses said. "Our coach has a black belt. We can't wake him."

Next thing you know we're sitting on a bed and we're surrounded by seven girls. Five of which are considerable; two are mugwumps. They're older than us and Steve passed me a bottle as we made introductions. I wrinkled my nose and forgot everyone's names. Steve took two swigs in a row. I hate alcohol. Don't need it.

"So what do you two do for fun in Fart Sniff?" one of the girls asks. She has a big nose and braces.

Steve looks to me. "We play Zombie."

"Zombie?" Big Glasses asks. She has a nice body.

"Zombie," Steve says. "Here, we'll show you" and he stands. I know he wants to do it to me, but I say no. I flick my wrist and that's our sign for no, *this is ours. Why share it?* He glances at me and looks back to the girls.

"We're waiting," one says. "Don't be cheap. You two are ambassadors for Fort Smurf."

They girls killed themselves laughing and rolling around on their beds. I wanted the one with cinnamon eyes. She must have been Gwichi'in. She had the same body as the one I saw in my first porno, so I know what she'd look like taking it hard. I'd like to stand close to her naked and feel her heat all over my face. I bet she'd look great under the red heat lamp in Steve's dad's sauna. I think I could tell her the truth as I finger her slowly as her eyes change colour: *I broke something. I did. I fucking hate myself for what I did to Brian. I do. Fuckin' forgive me, okay?* Maybe I could do this with Kelsey.

"Take it easy," Steve says. "You're from Gay River."

"At least we don't half kill transsexuals," Big Glasses says. The girls all go, "Ooooooh" and Steve looks at me and I blush and look down. I am suddenly ashamed. *We went too far. Why?*

"Why didn't you cut your hair?" one girl asks. "All the guys in Hay River did."

"And half the girls," another joins.

"I'm thinking about it," Steve says and this surprises me. Really? My eyes ask him but he's not looking at me anymore.

"Let's play truth or dare," one girl says. A brunette with a sharp nose.

"Uh oh," Big Glasses says. "Here comes the Sexpert."

Steve and I glance at each other.

"How do you jack off?" she asks and points at me. "You first. Then we'll all go."

Two of the girls bury their hands in their faces and start kicking the bed giggling and the others go, "Shh. Shh. Don't wake the coach." I suddenly love being here. I can smell perfume wafting from them and I see all their suitcases. And then I see her. There's a girl standing in the corner of a large closet with her nose in the corner. She is wearing her bra backwards—

pink and small—on the outside of her shirt. She has two Band-Aids on the back of the heels of her bare feet.

"Never mind her," Big Nose says. "Rebecca's being punished."

"Twat!" one of the girls hisses and they all laugh.

Steve gives me a look like we're in over our heads.

"I want to know," she says. "Sorry. We all want to know."

"Yeah," the girls all say. "How? How? Tell us."

Steve looks at me absolutely horrified. "Take it fuckin' easy. I'm not going to tell you."

"Okay, loser," one of the girls says. "I have a question about the gay boy."

Steve and I look at her.

"Rebecca's cousin says that police are investigating his father for holding him down and cutting off his hair."

Steve and I look at each other. "What?"

She nods. "Did his dad cut off his hair and then tie him up with his own clothes?"

"Where did you hear this?" I ask.

"It's on the news. We heard it on the way in."

"His dad didn't cut off his hair," Rebecca says softly.

"Shut it!" Big Nose says. "Speak ONLY when you are being spoken to or we'll make you do a lot more than you're already going to."

Rebecca nods. I'd love to see her face. Steve and I look at each other. So that's why he had short hair. *His dad?*

"Yeah," Lip Ring says, "my cousin said his dad had just got a call from a parent saying, 'Keep your It away from my kids.' Apparently, his folks didn't know he was leaving the house a boy and showing up to class a girl."

"How could you not know that?" Steve asks.

"So what was with the honey?" The Boss asks. "His dad covered him with honey?"

"No," Lip Ring says. "His Gran needed honey for some bannock and he had, like, four huge bottles."

"So, his dad tied him to a tree and poured four bottles of honey all over him while he was upside down?"

Breath spins in my throat as my face goes numb. I see sparks without any help from anyone as my stomach sinks. *So that's why he didn't run or fight back.* It must have been the day after. On the way to his Grandma's. Where we cut him off.

"Anyhow," one of the girls says, "we're thinking of ditching practice tomorrow to welcome him back to school."

"What do you mean?"

"He's out of the hospital tonight," the leader says. And she's watching us. She's onto us.

I glare at Steve. He's looking at his fingers. My face is burning.

"I'm bored," one of the girls says. "What is this Zombie?"

Steve gives me a dirty look and kicks off his dad's cowboy boot and pulls off his hockey sock and wraps it around his neck and pulls as he starts to huff. "I'll show you."

"No, wait. Steve—" I say because this is getting good. I need to know more about Brian.

Steve wraps his hockey sock around his neck so tight his neck veins bulge like strangling earth worms. He holds it and pulls harder. He starts to buck and twitch and the girls all backed away from him before he shot back and flew off the bed smacking his skull on the heater. A jet of blood sprayed the wall and the girls screamed. Steve starts to seizure and I grab him when the girls run for help. I push him through the window as the girls yell for their black belt coach. Steve landed on his neck on the pavement under the window and I drag him around the corner and hide behind the dumpster as he drooled and sputtered all over himself, and there was his bare foot all dusty now and his big toe nail's snapped up and blue. He came to and made the noises Johnny Knoxville made when Butterbean knocked him out with one punch in Jackass: "Gnnnhhh Gnnnuuuuhhhhhh."

It's the same sounds Brian made the last time I hurt him.

We cornered him in the bush. On his way home. He was carrying groceries from the Northern. It was honey. Four of the biggest bottles ever.

I was with Steve. "Cut your hair, hey, you little fag?"

It was true. Short hair only accentuated his features even more. His big eyes. He was gorgeous.

One look said it all. He looked down in complete surrender. He was dressed as a boy this time but I could see his earrings. We surrounded him. Started pushing him. "Why?" I'd push him over and over. "Why?" He was wearing lipstick and eye shadow.

"Why?"

"Yeah," Steve said and kicked him hard in the back. "Why?"

"Don't," I wanted to say. I'd never beaten Brian up with anyone else. I didn't like it. With Brian, I was the cat and he was the mouse. I loved making him cry. He was so fucking unreal it gave me pleasure hitting him, downing him. I pulled his pants off and was tempted to pull off his gonch but thought *no. Too much.* Steve ripped his shirt off his body and stomped him into the earth. I winced.

We ended tying Brian up upside down with his clothes to a tree. It was Steve's idea to pour the honey all over his legs, up his shorts, down his legs and leave him. I got so into it I didn't know. I didn't know the honey'd go into his mouth. I had no idea. He must have suffocated out there. Alone. In the bush. A mile from his home. But the thing is, next, he didn't scream. He didn't. Brian just looked away. As we beat him. As

I punched him so hard I connected with bone. I heard a pop. I can still hear the breath leaving his body as Steve stomped him in the chest.

And that's how we left him. I think I poured the honey all over him, but I want to say it was Steve. Upside down. Brian looking away, crying quietly but no tears, honey searching his body. He'd shaved his legs. I felt the stubble when I held him and we used his shirt and jacket as rope.

I had no fucking idea honey would pool towards his mouth.

An hour later at the landslide. That's when I heard the ambulance. We were drinking, smoking, passing a mickey back and forth *and I knew.*

I knew it was for him.

I was secretly worried when we walked away. I thought he'd get down. Wiggle his way out. I had no idea the honey would hunt for his mouth and nose, that he'd drown that way. That no matter how much he panicked and shook his head back and forth, the honey would pool to find inside his nostrils, mouth and eyes.

So why the fuck didn't he run? I wondered. Why didn't he struggle?

We'd crucified him upside down with honey and that was the night after—when I dare myself to think about it—that was the night after his father held him down and cut off all his hair.

Keep your 'It' away from my kid.

Brian didn't run because his heart was broken. What did he have left?

We were his final humiliation.

It was Mr. Murray who'd found him. Walking his dog. It was Mr. Murray who pulled him down and scooped the honey out of his throat, his nose. His wife is a nurse. Mr. Murray volunteers for the ambulance. His wife used her mouth to suck the honey out of his nose. They say his lips were blue. Brian's eyes were fused shut. He was deaf. The honey was swelling inside his skull.

As the coach comes running outside holding the longest flashlight in human history, I pull Steve deeper into shadows. I go, "Shhhhhhh," "Shhh," "Shh." I hold him and he sags into me. I get a waft of warm air off his body and smell his pit-stick: *Cinnamon.*

"We went too far," I finally say.

Steve comes to and asks, "Where's my boot?"

Today, it's quarter to nine. Brian always arrives at quarter to nine. It's his first day back. He comes in and he is bald. He must have shaved it all off. Or maybe the nurses. Or his mom.

Brian's wearing lipstick this morning. He is so beautiful. Even more beautiful than ever. Even with a black eye and a limp. Is it his doe-eyes, his sharp nose, or how slender he is?

I look around and everyone, including me, has cut their hair. Hundreds of us. As Brian walks towards the foyer, we all stand. He stops and looks around and sees all the students and the teachers who have cut their hair off.

Steve's not here. The pigs were at his house this morning. I saw the Paddy Wagon and turned around.

Why? I ask myself. I would always ask Brian that, but there's no way he could answer. He could never have known what I was really asking him. I cut all my hair off this morning. I want him to see me like this. I need him to see me like this. There's Kelsey. She's shaved all her red hair off and looks so tiny, like a bird. A swallow. She's beside him now. She's crying, touching his eye. And there's the police. The Paddy Wagon pulls right up to the foyer. Shit! I can almost see Steve in the backseat. I wonder if he's cut his hair. I bet you a million dollars he's looking at his fingers.

And there's the volleyball team from last night. Big Nose, Big Glasses and The Sexpert have cut their hair short. The man beside Big Nose looks in my direction and he looks tough. Mean. He starts to make his way towards me the exact moment I see two RCMP members come through the door. They spot me.

I have seconds left. I have to move fast. I look at Brian and start clapping first. Brian looks at me. For a second, he is confused. He squints. When he focuses and sees it's me, I pray he sees my haircut. I did it last night as soon as I got home. Dad was waiting. He was like, "Ronny, fuck sakes anyways. Why do the cops keep calling the house?"

I chopped my hair off by myself and didn't even care how I looked. "It's about Steve. He did something dumb," I called as my hair feathered the sink and my shoulders.

Brian looks my way. He looks my way as the RCMP and the coach with the black belt approach and corral me. I'm all out of time. I broke something beautiful and hate myself for it. I am clapping as loud as I can before the school catches on. As Brian looks my way, I can tell he is confused, but he is thinking. He is thinking about when I last looked into his eyes as I punched and swung and punched him again and again as he went down. I think he read my mind. As hard as I swung and as hard as I hit he must have seen it in my eyes: the question and the answer to my *Why?*

Why, Brian? Why the fuck are you so beautiful, and why have I always wanted you so much?

Where are you tonight?

Juliet Hope is alone and lonely and the moon is the light of ache and if-only. I want a baby. I want a baby. *I want a baby. Even with my eyes closed I want one. To be full. To never be alone again. To raise and hold. To be one with someone. The world will leave me alone then. And it can be just us. We can play all day and I can watch you grow. It will be just us and I'll never have to share my love with anyone else again. With babies, you can start over, and I already love you, she thinks. I already do. She thinks of Darcy. That was a mistake. One day out of my life. One time and I've got him if I need him. There's Larry, the puppy dog. Always watching me. Always wondering, I am sure, what I'd be like. And then there's the new boy: Johnny. God, he's gorgeous. He's beautiful. That face. Those eyes. Those hands. He's kind. I can tell. A girl knows. He's almost the one.*

Why have I never had a girlfriend? she wonders. Oh. I know. It's because I'm a threat. Always have been. Even when I was little, I could tell women hated me. How their husbands watched me grow. How the principal and gym teacher and Mr. Harris watch me now.

She touches her tummy, sweeps her hands slowly over herself. *Soon, my baby. Soon.*

Junior races home from pumping gas at Norm's, the only gas station in Fort Simmer. *This is it,* he thinks. *This is it!* For the past two months, someone's been playing with his stereo and cranking his tunes. He knows it's Karen. Just knows it. He's hidden his speaker cables in his room, but they're never put back the way he'd left them. He's given his sister heck, but she denies, denies, denies. "You're gonna blow my speakers!" he yells at her, but she swears it isn't her. Junior's been making money on the side at the teen dances as a DJ. Two hundred bucks cash on the dash every Friday and he knows what packs the dance floor. He's got a system: Hip Hop, Dance, Techno, Country—repeat—

He races home an hour earlier than he told his family he'd be because tonight's the night: he's going to catch her doing this. She's been spending too much time at home now that she got barred from the Pinebough. Halfway up Ptarmigan, he kills the lights on his truck and coasts two houses down. He slams it in park and gets out, starts running. Sure enough, he can hear the house shaking with the bass! Karen's cranking the tunes so much the house is booming and bumping. *She's gonna blow my speakers!*

Junior picks up the pace. He can't place the song, but it's drum thunder and brutally loud. *This is it!* he thinks. This is finally it. I'm gonna catch her and she's gonna get it! But what is that song?

He races into his house and opens the door with a "Jeezus, Karen!" when he catches his dad, Reggie, dancing with his shirt off. Reggie is in his blue long johns and dancing up a storm, hopping up and down with his eyes closed, his arms twirling, and it's not a song Junior owns. It's his dad's music. It's Hand games music.

Whoe whoe whoe whoe whoe whoe
yah yah yah yah
whoe whoe whoe whoe whoe
yah yah yah yah ...

His dad's supposed to be hunting but he's home. Junior freezes and sees his dad hopping around to the Hand games music. He can hear the hypnotic drumming of twelve men hammering twelve caribou drums all singing in this rhythm that staggers Junior's breathing because it's so powerful and loaded with medicine. His blood roars and his eyes cross with the feelings he gets when he watches his dad play Hand games.

Reggie has this move where he flutters his hands like ptarmigan wings in front of the opposing team as he makes a "hass" sound to confuse them, and he's doing it now: "Hass, hass, hass."

The drums boom over and over. He can hear the spruce drum sticks pound the skins and his dad, topless and free, is singing along, eyes closed, wiggling his hips, hopping up and down with his big grown arms up like Hulk Hogan after a body slam. Man, Junior thinks as he switches from outrage to shock. Dad can really move.

When he first started to play last year, he looked like a big baby wearing water wings hopping up and down in a Jolly Jumper. As soon as Junior thinks that, his dad opens his eyes, drops his arms and covers his nipples, his little belly, back and forth, back and forth.

"Dad?" Junior mouths.

The drumming and singing are still blaring. It's a live recording and Junior can hear people whoop it up as they watch the drum competition. His dad has a little moustache now and the shadow of a goatee. His hair has grown and his cheeks are burnt from the wind.

Junior looks down out of respect and doesn't know if he should leave or what. His dad scrambles out of the kitchen and races into Mom's sewing room. Junior stands there and closes his eyes. *What did I just see?* He tries to find lyrics to the chanting and singing but it's that "Whoe whoe whoe whoe whoe whoe yah yah yah yah whoe whoe whoe whoe whoe yah yah yah yah ..." times a hundred.

Junior has never seen his dad dance and he marvels at what a strong body his dad has. It's been forever since they shared anything. His dad's been hard on him this past year: more chores, more expectations, more demands. *And here he is: Dad's the one! I've gone after Karen all this time for cranking my tunes, but it's been Dad?*

Reggie comes out of the sewing room with his favourite red AC/DC T-shirt on, blushing and laughing, before going into Junior's room to kill the tunes.

Junior stands there in the porch and sees his dad out of breath and embarrassed. He's actually blushing when he says, "Uh, hi." He starts laughing again and clasps his hands once— as if to clear the air.

"I thought you were hunting," Junior says.

"I was, but we got called home. Our team made it to the Dene Hand games Competition in Rae."

"Wow."

"You should come with me," his dad says. "I could teach you." He's trying to be serious but bursts out laughing again and Junior can see that his dad's ears are purple. It's been years since his dad has laughed out of embarrassment and

Junior starts laughing with him. He starts laughing so hard and can see his dad walking towards him. His dad's still wearing his blue long johns and a gonch underneath, thank God. His dad hugs him and they laugh together. "That's your grandfather's song," his dad says and Junior holds his father, feels his whiskers against him. "Come with me." His dad smells of smoke and the land. *He's smoking again*, Junior thinks. *I won't tell Mom.* He closes his eyes and grabs his dad with a hug and a wish and a *Thank you, God, for this.*

"Okay," he says to his father and he can still hear that song: the song of his grandfather.

Kevin Garner is trying to listen to his Granny as she spreads her Bingo sheets out. She's talking. More stories. Half English. Half Dogrib. She's got two Bingo dabbers ready to go and her lucky statue of the Virgin Mary that glows in the dark. As a kid, he used to watch the statue when he'd sleep on the couch, and he was convinced it levitated towards him ever so slowly throughout the night. It used to scare him so much that he'd half pray and half blubber to her, "Let me live, Virgin Mary! Let me live. Do it for Jesus. Please. My Granny needs me. She needs me. Who'll take care of her if I die young? Plus you're a virgin and holy. Don't be cheap and kill me. If you kill me you're cheap, okay? "

As much as his Granny loved the church, Kevin never trusted it. He still didn't understand The Trinity and he did not believe that Jesus died for his sins. He thought the classic northern baptism was having your bike stolen; he thought the classic confirmation was when you got your first hickey. He also thought Grandma's bannock fresh out of the oven was his Communion.

He shakes his head thinking about this and, now, here he is: older, with his Granny talking and trusting him with stories about the old ways, about how a bear always knows what you're thinking, about how it's the dragonfly who can move through the four worlds. Her English is getting better as his Dogrib limps along. He's listening and sees she's been using her Bingo dabber to mark her days on the calendar. *What is she waiting for?* he wonders.

She is talking about how she used beaver castors to save his uncle's leg. How she cut each one into four under the full moon before doctoring him.

He's listening and wonders what he's missing tonight. There's a party at The Maze, for sure. *Maybe Juliet will be there, maybe not. She's already got eyes for Johnny, he thinks. I can't believe she and Darcy McMannus humped. How cheap. Darcy "Mc- Anus"? What a lump!* His Granny has twenty sheets out and he sees that she's offering him to play four, for luck. "Nah," she says.

"*Ehtsi,*" he says. "I'm going out."

He's made her tea. She has her bannock and jam and butter. He's boiled three eggs for her and set aside salt and pepper, the big spoon for cracking, the knife for sawing and the little spoon for eating. He's boiled the eggs for four minutes exactly and now they're cooling in a bowl. She eats them cold with a pile of salt and pepper. She'll be fine tonight. He's made her a pot of tea, which she'll sip with a ton of sugar and cream from a can.

"*Nah,*" she offers him her Bingo dabber again. "*Ho.*"

"*In leh,*" he says. "I gotta go, *Ehtsi.*"

"Where?" she says. "To another party?"

He can't lie to her. "Granny, don't be like that. I'm young. I wanna go out."

"I dreamt of a white dragonfly last night," she says.

"Oh?" he asks. This is new.

"It's you," she says. "It's good luck. We'll win tonight. I can feel it."

"How?" Kevin asks. There's his coat. His shoes. He's got forty bucks. Enough to go Bazook.

"Itchy palms," she says and holds them up. "Come on, you. We'll split the jackpot and eat Cheezies."

Kevin grins. *"Ehtsi,"* he says. "You keep it."

"Twenty grand," his granny looks at him and beams.

"What?"

She nods. "They're raising money for the Handi Bus. Some *moonyow* crashed it and now they need a new door for the wheelchair lift."

"Twenty grand," he says. "Seriously?"

She nods. *"Heh eh. Sombah cho.* We'll split it. Come you, my white dragonfly."

Twenty grand, Kevin thinks. *Ten thousand reasons to stay in.* He looks out the window and sees the cars and trucks whizzing by. *You can feel it,* Kevin thinks. *Friday night. This town loves to party and I can feel it.*

His granny holds out her Bingo dabber to him. *She's lonely,* he thinks. *All her friends are gone.*

He goes to her, takes the Bingo dabber, kisses the top of her forehead and smiles. "Okay, Granny. I'll stay, but if I win, you have to let me buy you breakfast tomorrow at the café."

"Deal," she smiles.

Kevin sits beside her and touches her hand as he takes the Bingo dabber. *A white dragonfly, huh?* he thinks. *And*

ten grand? That's a lot of booze, a lot of pot. Maybe a truck.
Maybe a trip to Edmonton, to West Ed. That's a lot of action.
Maybe my new Amazement Plan starts tonight.

"I love you, Granny," he says. "Even if we don't win."

"Oh we'll win. These itchy palms never lie. They were itchy
the night I met Alphonse and they were itchy the night you
were born." She wrinkles her nose at him and pushes him
lightly. "You grew up so fast."

He looks at his four sheets as the local town station switches from Fort Simmer community announcements to the live
broadcast of the Bingo. Kevin thinks about how he and the TV
are his Granny's only friends. She turns it on first thing every
day for company. She hardly goes out anymore and her only
visitor now is the nurse, to check up on her.

Kevin's palms start to itch and burn and he looks at them,
marvels at them.

"See?" his Granny says. "Feel them?"

He looks at his hands and then he looks at her. "Yes. Yes!
I feel them."

"I told you," she says and smiles. "Good luck."

Johnny Beck is in awe of his looks as he works out, and he
loves the aroma of his own musk. It's the smell of his uncles
after they hunt and the memory of his father carrying him
when he used to pretend to be asleep. Johnny's arms are tight
after seven reps of preacher curls, and he loves how he looks
in the mirror. He flexes and hears Donny stir and call for him
in his sleep. Johnny makes sure his little brother is okay before
taking another moment to admire himself in his mother's full-
length mirror. *Is it my eyes? Is it my smile?* A thought hits

him, a realization: *You know what I need?* he thinks. I need an *"in." someone to get me closer to Juliet Hope, past the mugwumps. I need an apostle, so who's the sucker? Who's it gonna be?* Donny stirs again and Johnny watches, listens. *He's had way too much sugar tonight.* "I will do better tomorrow, buddy," he whispers. Johnny surveys his mother's bedroom. It's filthy. *What a pig,* he thinks. And all of a sudden it comes to him: Larry Sole. That lost little boy of a man who always sits alone and is always watching Juliet. *Yes, let it be him who gets me to her.* He catches his reflection in the mirror again and smiles. *Ladies,* he thinks. *It's not even fair what I have. Not. Even. Fair.*

Darcy McMannus is spinning. His thoughts are slow and looming as he watches the red glow of the hot knives die.

"Do you want me to?" Jazz asks.

"What?"

"Do you want me to?"

"No." He sits up—or tries to. He's so tired, so wasted, so done.

"You sure?"

"Yeah, don't."

"But it's fun."

"Don't," Darcy commands Jazz with his eyes, or tries to. *Who does Jazz think he is? There was a time I never had to repeat myself.*

"I'm gonna," Jazz says, rolling up his sleeve.

"What did I just say?" Darcy says again. *Who the eff does Jazz think he is? Since last summer, Jazz has become more cunning, more ... sinister.*

"Try and stop me," Jazz grins.

Darcy tries to stand but he's too stoned. He slurs something that sounds like it came from somebody behind him.

Jazz starts to giggle. Then he starts to bray.

The Jackal, Darcy thinks. They call Jazz the Jackal because of that laugh. It's a half screech or half howl, like something wild and on fire running through the night.

"I can't," Darcy wheezes. "I can't stand."

"That was more than a joint," Jazz says. "I put a little magic in there. A little—how you say—hibiscus?"

"What?" Darcy realizes. "What did we just smoke?"

Jazz reaches into the fish tank and grabs Fishy, the pregnant fish—Darcy's favourite. "Watch," he says.

"Don't!" Darcy reaches. He sees his own hand. It's meant for power and to punish and crush. Now it can only reach. He feels little. Jazz squeezes Fishy hard. Fishy explodes into a pink fleshy mist and hundreds of pink somethings are born through Jazz's fingers.

"I'm a god," Jazz says and roars with laughter. "I just made a million babies in my name. They were born through me and already sing my name."

Darcy focuses on what's left of the mother. Her mouth moves, gasping once. One of her eyes has pushed out sideways and is looking right at him.

"Jesus!" Darcy flushes and sinks into the couch. *I will never tell anyone about this, especially Juliet. What would she say? What would she think of me? Juliet, where are you? he wonders. Help me!*

"What you're thinking about, D?" Jazz asks as he examines his dripping hand. Things are moving between his fingers. Baby fish. They either have tails or long fins. "Hey. They tickle."

Darcy weaves. "When I get up—"

"What are you gonna do?" Jazz approaches him. "Here. Smell this."

Jazz smears his fingers all over and inside Darcy's nose and nostrils.

Darcy's skull is filled with an ocean he's only seen in pictures and on TV. It's sweet and sour and his nostrils are moving. From the inside. Those babies—the living tissue of them—are inside his nose and crawling up!

Jazz scream-laughs in Darcy's face as Darcy pinches his nose to snuff it out. It's moving, wriggling, but he can't even lift his arms. He's stoned. Body stoned. And now sleepy. The baby fish are crawling up his nose, they're inside his skull.

He realizes he's crying, sobbing. *Why can't I move?*

Jazz flips the fish tank over, and the other fish Darcy loves spill onto the carpet. Jazz starts jumping up and down on each one as it tries to wriggle away. "Juliet was mine!" he screams. "She was supposed to be all mine!"

God, Darcy prays. Get me out of here!

Larry Sole has wings but only he can see them. *Wait. That's not true. Maybe Juliet can see them when she catches me watching her, he thinks. She watches me, too. I can feel it. She must know that I am the Ambassador of Love. I am a soldier of passion.* He is out past the highway, standing quietly in the middle of a dog team. Huskies. Some of them are half wolf. All of them are sleeping. He's slipped through them all. He's learned to put his spirit into the back pocket of his jeans so no one or nothing can sense him. Jed told him about how the Slavey used to be able to do this before battle and he's doing it now. *What is the new kid Johnny doing right now? he wonders. What is Juliet up to tonight? Or Darcy and Jazz—I wonder who's the most dangerous of them all? The husky to his right stirs and quiets. When will Jed come home? There was a trapper who came by an hour ago but it wasn't Jed. Jed's Tundra doesn't have a rifle rack. Mom's studying. I'll make her bannock when I go home. That always cheers her up. Oh, but then she'll see my tattoo.*

Larry had spent the afternoon drawing a love spell on his right hand: for Juliet Hope.

She will fall in love with me tonight, he thinks. She will. Even from this distance, this distance between us. It's shrinking. I know you can feel it, Juliet. With invisible ink and a raven feather, I have created love medicine for us. I have a triangle on my palm to show the three emotions you feel when you find love: faith, hope and attraction. There's a leaf with roots underneath the triangle because it represents growth, and I drew two hearts with a line joining them and that's a star above the triangle because it represents beauty. There's three throwing stars to defend us because this town loves to tear happy couples apart. There's a peace sign because we should feel peace when we're in love and there's a box coloured in because love is like winning Black Out Bingo when it's shared. There's a boomerang so our love will always come back stronger, and I drew a heart alone so if anyone tries to take Juliet away from me it won't work for them, and I drew an infinity circle and an amethyst to capture the light of the world and even the northern lights, and I drew a baby raven to honour the feather of this spell because I heard ravens can grow to be a hundred years old so our love will last a hundred years easy. Even if Juliet can't see my hand, I know she can feel it. Juliet, when you and I kiss, the night will explode into fire and angels. Even if I never have the chance to make love to you, I will always praise you. I will always adore you. I will always cherish you in everything I do from this moment on. You are the reason I was born. Where God's hands never went, I can reach that place for you. They say love is a thunder and I feel it in my everything for you. My love for you is so loud that it's practically bubonic. I raise my fist and swear it.

And that's when the huskies wake up.

The Strongest Blood

That first August after Joey and Leo had graduated from PWS High School, Leo's father, Isadore, took the boys out grouse hunting with a .410 outside of Wood Buffalo National Park— 23 kilometers from Fort Simmer in the Northwest Territories of Canada. Leo knew that his mother, Dora, wanted him and his cousin Joey to attend Aurora College, and that today was the day his dad was supposed to lobby both young men to attend the college in September.

"Dad, I'm 17. I don't want to be a social worker or get into office administration," Leo shivered as he and Joey walked alongside his father's truck. Both Leo and Joey were tired and cold. Leo'd forgotten his long johns. Joey was even colder. With his low-rider gangster pants, everyone could see Joey's gonch. Isadore had insisted on leaving the house by seven to get the most grouse and chickens, and now they could hear Joey's teeth chatter. Joey agreed. "I don't want to operate heavy equipment and I'm not into nursing or being a teacher. We want to make money."

"We want our own trucks," Leo said.

Isadore slowed the truck and rolled down his window. Both boys turned to see what he saw. "Wallow pit," Isadore said and pointed with his chin.

Leo pretended to be interested. He'd already walked by a few this morning when hunting for grouse, and the pits were all pretty rank. The wood bison would urinate on a spot and then roll around in it. Part of this, Leo knew, was to get all musky as this was prime mating season for the bison, and the other part was to get dusty enough to keep the bugs away.

Joey had wrinkled his nose when he first caught the scent and actually dry heaved. "Whoah! Get your stink on, or what!" he yelled.

"Shhhh," Leo scolded him, trying to act all serious, but then burst out laughing. "We gotta be quiet, *you*."

Joey plugged his nose and waved his hand in front of his face. "Ever rank, hey?"

Leo looked around. He could see tufts of bison hair in the rose bushes. Fresh droppings and hoofed tracks were everywhere. Maybe today was the day Joey got to see the bison up close. Leo's parents brought Joey down from Wha Ti because now that the diamond mines were in full swing in the north, his parents were drinking far more than Joey needed to be around, Dora said. "There!" Joey said and fired on a grouse.

Leo looked. It was a headshot. Joey went to retrieve his target. "Supper!"

Leo looked back to Isadore, who was sitting in the truck, and smiled. The fall colours were upon the leaves of the birch, so the forest behind Isadore was yellow and orange. Leo stopped and took in the visual splendor of the bush. Isadore flashed his lights and waved. Leo wished he'd remembered to take a camera because this was something he never wanted to forget. Even though he was cold, the sun was rising, and the air was sweet as the frost left the grass, leaves and trees.

Leo was surprised at what a great shot Joey was. Isadore wanted the boys to compete to see who could line up more grouse with one shot, but Leo could only do that with ptarmigan. As far as Leo saw, grouse travelled alone, while the ptarmigan packed up in the winter.

"Anyhow," Isadore said as the boys got back into the truck, "your mom wants you to get an education. You know that."

"We do," Leo held his hands over the hot air vent, "and we will, but right now we need to make money, and I want to learn Dogrib."

His dad nodded as he thought about it. "Come on," he said. "Let's cruise."

The truck picked up speed and they made their way towards the Park.

Ever since Fort Simmer hosted a sun dance four years in a row, Dene culture had come back with a force: there were now tea dances, drum dances, Hand games, singing groups and storytelling nights at the museum that all packed in the people. It was like the town had been in hiding from its own inheritances as Aboriginal people and northerners living side by side. Someone had even spray-painted, "It is time to learn from the Red Man—IDLE NO MORE!" on the water tower in huge black letters that could be seen from the bank and drugstore.

Leo watched his dad. It was no secret that Isadore was a champion card player and had won Benny the Bank's house in a poker game one night. He'd never gone to collect, but the story spread like wildfire as Benny was one of the most dangerous men in the north. It was a good thing that he was in jail.

What did Mom always say? he sighed. This town is so full of the wrong kind of heroes.

Leo closed his eyes and wondered what his graduating class was up to. What were Larry, Johnny, Juliet, Kevin, Darcy and Jazz the Jackal up to?

Leo had had a dream one night of holding a leash that held a two-headed black bear. It was powerful. Both heads swung and bit the air in front of them and he realized as he woke up that the leash was sinew made from flesh and human hair. It was slick with gut slime.

"Oooh," he said as he shivered. He turned his hands into fists and stretched. He had to warm up. Why did everyone he grew up with know what they wanted to do with their lives while he didn't? The streakers: Grant, Brutus, Clarence. They were finding their way in the world one night run at a time. How did they discover their trails in the night? What drove them?

Leo shook his head. This world and his future was a mystery. He just didn't know what he wanted to do or be.

They were driving slowly over a hill when Isadore drew his breath in fast and stopped his truck.

"What, Dad?" Leo asked.

Isadore nodded and pointed quickly with his lips.

"Whoah," Joey said in a whisper.

Down the hill walked a herd of six bison cows led by a strong bull. Leo watched in awe at how the bull trotted, easily handling its bulky body, with a hump that must have been six feet high. The bull's thick head was black but the rest of the body was brown. The herd's breath rose together.

Walking towards them was another younger bull with eight cows. The junior bull was smaller than the older bull. Both stopped when they got close enough.

"Get out of the truck quietly." Isadore pulled out a pair of binoculars from the glove box. "Don't slam your doors."

Leo and Joey did as they were told. Joey was out first, and he put his hands over his brow to block out the rising sun. Leo did the same.

Isadore motioned for the boys to hunch down so the bison would not see or smell them. Leo crouched and Joey knelt. Leo squinted and took a good hard look at the older bull whose beard and chaps were fuller. Thick black horns shone in the sun and the older bull stood perfectly still as he waited for the younger one to come closer.

The younger bull walked with a raised head towards his elder and his cows stopped before he did. It was almost as if they knew what was going to happen before anyone else, including the men. Three ravens flew from the west and perched themselves on the tallest spruce across the highway. Leo shook his head at them. If they were here, he thought, this would get serious.

The older bull looked back once to the lead cow in his harem and motioned towards the bush to the left. The lead cow did as she was told and walked off with the five other cows and they stood quietly together.

The younger bull did the same. His cows walked off to his right.

"Wolves," Isadore whispered. "Look at their tails."

Leo saw the tails on two of the cows belonging to the older bull. They looked like extension cords without their natural hide. Wolves had chased two of the cows and had yanked so hard on their tails with their teeth that they'd pulled off their fur and skin. No wonder, Leo thought, the cows did not walk with yearlings. The wolves must have taken them all. Leo imagined the older bull goring the wolves with his horns or kicking them with his powerful hooves.

Leo suddenly wished his mom was there with them so she could see this, but she'd not been feeling well and had told them to leave her behind.

The last time they'd all gone for a family cruise, they passed by a bull with only a snub for a tail. "Look at that!" Leo had said as he sat up in the backseat.

The snub of the bull's tail had looked like a little black finger wriggling around. "Oh, how he must suffer with the bugs," Dora had said.

"Get ready, boys," Isadore said, and Leo could hear the excitement in his voice. Leo looked to his dad. Isadore was so happy that, for a second, he seemed young again. Strong. He looked to Joey who squinted out of habit whenever he got excited. Leo looked at Joey's braces, and when he saw his cousin's smile and shining eyes, he was suddenly filled with so much love for Joey his blood warmed in his back and shoulders.

The two bulls stood like gods on four legs opposing each other. They lowered their heads at the same time, their beards brushing the frost. The bulls started pawing the earth. The younger bull let out a jet of piss and the older raised his massive head quickly to catch its scent.

"Who's the toughest, Leo?" Joey asked out loud. "The one with more experience or the youngest?"

"Sometimes the biggest isn't the toughest," Leo said, eyeing the smaller bull.

"It's the strongest who's gonna win this," Isadore answered and both bulls charged, raising their heads and slamming them together. It took a split second before the sound hit as a solid, "*Ca rack!*"

The sound was so loud one of the ravens jumped up and soared before landing again on a spruce bough directly above the battleground. The other two ravens followed and the spruce boughs swayed as they landed on them.

The bulls pushed against each other and, at first, no bull gave ground, but soon the older bull fell backwards. Leo was surprised to see tufts of fur rise and float in the air.

"Ho-la," Joey said.

"Fur, no less," Leo said.

All of the cows watched quietly, patient and still. Only their rising breath or a tail flip gave away their perfect stillness.

The bulls stopped and backed up. They were going to charge again.

"Twenty bones on the young one," Joey said and started rubbing his hands together. "How about whoever loses buys lunch."

"Shhh," Leo said.

"Deal," Isadore said, and Leo looked at both Joey and his father. They were smiling. Because of his father's twisted fingers, Isadore couldn't shake hands properly, but it was understood: the bet was solid. Leo shook his head, grinned, and went back to staring at the bison.

The bulls started off the same as before, rising like rams before a head butt, but this time the older bull swung his head low and to the right under the younger one, digging his left horn under the younger bull's right leg. The younger bull had not anticipated this, overshot his mark, and was now off balance. The older bull lifted the top half of the younger's body off the ground and began digging his horn into the other's nerve bed, shredding tendons and ligaments in the pit of the leg. The men heard the younger bull cry out in a wail, a man's voice, and Leo winced, imagining the gristle popping, and then it was over.

"Hooked 'im," Isadore said.

The older bull dropped the younger bull, but when the younger bull landed on his front hooves, his left hoof would not work. It froze like a horse's wooden leg on a carousel.

"Holy shit!" Joey said.

"Did you see that?" Leo asked stupidly.

Isadore was silent and watched the scene though the binoculars.

The older bull had pushed the younger one off the road into the ditch with his horns and now the younger one could only hop on three legs to maintain his balance.

"Paralyzed him," Isadore said.

Leo looked at his dad and suddenly felt sick. He looked at Joey who had his mouth open. Leo suddenly felt very cold. "Just like that?"

Isadore nodded. "Just like that."

The older bull looked at his harem and nodded. All six cows moved together. They walked as one, a herd of muscle and power past the younger bull who hopped in the ditch, alone. The younger bull tried to hop his way back on the road but couldn't.

The older bull and his cows passed the younger bull's eight cows and, without a motion that Leo could see, the younger bull's cows joined the tail end of the older bull's harem.

"Fourteen cows," Joey yelled. "Fourteen cows! Not bad for a morning's work, eh?"

The junior bull stood still, stood shivering, breathing heavily, its tongue hanging out of its mouth, while the older bull walked away with fourteen cows behind him.

Leo looked at the ravens. One was watching him, Leo thought, with human eyes. The ravens spread their wings and dropped down closer, jumping to the spruce boughs below, getting closer to the bull.

"The old bull played weak, hey?" Isadore said. "I used to do that."

"What?" Leo asked.

"When I used to play cards, I played weak if I had pocket aces or a full house." He looked to his son. "Sometimes you gotta play weak to get what you want."

"Hunh," Leo said and nodded.

"What'll happen now?" Joey asked.

"Wolves," Isadore said.

Leo nodded. "Want to go home and get your .30/30?"

Leo saw Isadore and Joey both look at the .410 Joey had beside him. "No. We're in the park. The wolves will get him."

"That's it?" Leo asked as he took one last look at the lone bull with its dead leg.

"That's it," his father answered. "Let's go for lunch. Joey's buying."

"Wha!" Joey said. "I'm seventeen and buying lunch? Cheap!"

"Deal's a deal," Isadore said, and winked at Leo.

Leo looked back at the trees. The raven that had been watching him was now sharpening its beak on a branch.

Fort Simmer, his dad often told him, was a place of survival and miracles. Anything can happen anytime. The outlaws, Torchy and Sfen, were on the run. He used to fear them. They burned down thirty homes months ago and the town was now starting to rebuild. His dad had thought he'd seen one of them—probably Torchy—scurrying across the highway one night coming home, but maybe it was a wolverine.

He thought of the young bull, in the ditch, all alone. This would be his last day alive, as soon, the wolves would come.

Leo promised himself that when he got back to town, he'd ask his mother for tobacco. They would pray together for the grouse, the buffalo, and the wolves. Then they would talk about his future.

I Double Dogrib Dare You

I keep waking up holding things.

I haven't told anyone. But I do.

One time it was a shell-casing recently fired; another time it was a butterfly wing the colour of rust.

Brutus and Clarence don't know, and tonight I sit with the one I secretly call "Holy Woman."

"Witch," a woman hissed at her as she walked by.

"Skinny ass," another said.

I winced.

Valentina's hair would feel like feathers in the dark.

The DJ had somehow managed to overheat the system so the music wasn't on, but the lights were off and the candlelight on the tables made everything glow. Gunner and his troglodytes were giving me the stink eye from across the room, and I was scared. Really scared. Our court date was set. I bet I could let Country, the bouncer, know about the restraining order if I had to, but that would mean passing Gunner's table and that would expose my legs. Would they do it here? I bet they would: to teach Fort Smith a lesson.

"So what will you do now?" I asked. She looked down and this was my chance to study her. There was that foxlike nose. There was that naturally feathered hair. All these years and she hadn't changed. In fact, she looked younger. Her dress was gorgeous. She was so fancy. You could tell the dress was from anywhere but here. She was elegance. She was grace. And she hadn't aged in any of the pictures I'd found of her in the Catholic diocese archives going back eighty years.

"I'm not sure," she looked away. "Sell the house."

Whoah. Talk about the end of an era. If anyone other than her or her family owned that house all by itself down the highway, that'd be the end of so many great memories. Valentina was a foster child who'd lost both her foster mom and dad this past year. She came home for both funerals and I was out of town both times. Brutus and Clarence said she stole the show with her beauty, but she never cried. Both funerals, they said, and she never cried.

"What about you?" she asked.

"I don't know," I said. "The boss's sick. He needs help."

She took a sip of water. "So you're doing what again?"

"He got the contract to install water barrels around town, but he's sick. His heart..."

"Rain barrels?"

"Yeah. Everyone's worried about the water in the Slave, so the town figures we could trust the rainwater for our gardens."

"Wow, so you're doing that and driving the elders around?"

"Yeah," I said. "I guess I'm the only one around here without a criminal record and a class 5." I paused. "Wah!"

She smiled. "Do you love it?"

"I do," I nodded. "I seriously do."

"But I read in the paper you got charged?"

She read the papers? "Yeah. Gunner over there—don't look—was stealing from the elders and I caught him."

"So why are you being charged?"

I decide to go for it. "I held him down and got the elders to call the cops. He says I assaulted him, but I have twelve elders now who'll come to the JP with me and testify that Gunner's been stealing meat from them from the community hunts."

She shot Gunner a dirty look. "You're kidding me."

"Nope," I said. "He's been taking the back straps, ribs, thighs. Even moose-nose and the Bible. He's been robbing them all for years but everyone's been too scared to talk."

She looked his way. "I'm so sad to hear this."

I remembered holding him down. It was only luck that I got him. I kept pushing his head and neck into the corner of the room while calling for help. "This is your last chance," he kept saying. "Grant, let me go."

But I knew if I did he'd half kill me.

So I couldn't.

I just kept kneeling on him and twisting his neck back and he couldn't move. He kept trying to flip me but I buried my palms into his face and neck so that I had razor burn on my palms for days.

I caught Valentina reading me so I blurted, "Yeah," I said. "But I love what I do. The elders here have a long memory." I watched her eyes on this one. I was testing her.

"Yup..." She looked away and I studied her lips. I made out with her a few times when we were in our teens and the Purple Cow movie theatre was up and running, and we had the Bowling Alley. I never forgot how her bottom lip shivered when I kissed her, how she poured herself into me with her heat each time. She once told me she loved that scar I have inside my lower lip. It's a bumpy ridge I still trace when I'm thinking or start to get tired. I got it from a rock fight with Torchy and

: FISH
: MacKinnon, Patricia Joan
:
3906515231
8273
Transited: September 12, 2019 1: 42 PM

Sfen when we were kids and it's actually a blessing. Women love it for all the right reasons. It's like a second tongue.

"That was a great reunion, hey?" I said.

"Shari did a great job."

"Twenty years…"

"I know."

"Twenty years," I said, "and some things don't change." Again, I was testing her. My Grandpa, before he died, warned me about her. He said when he was a boy, she was here. Even in his nineties he warned me to watch out for her, that she was half spirit. She came to us as an orphan, he said, and the men she married all died young. He showed me a picture of my Grandma taken in 1921 on Treaty Day and Valentina was standing behind her looking left. She was still the same. Young. Beautiful. But it was something he said, in his own words, that I never forgot: "She sings the snow."

I didn't know what he meant. He said a lot of things before he passed, but that's the one I think about most now.

"You've got some new moves," she smiled. "Want to dance when they get going?"

"Sure," I said. I got the JP to show me how he and his wife two-stepped so good, and he made me put on a pair of wool socks at his house. He and his wife pushed all their furniture to the wall and, in four minutes, they had me dosey-doeing around their living room like nothin'. Holy cow! "So what are you up to now?"

"I'm not sure."

"There was supposed to be a party at the Towers."

"I know. The rain makes everything cheap."

"Oh, now, it's just drizzle. What about you?"

She sighed. "I leave first thing but I'm not tired."

"Oh?" I got the tinglies. Maybe this was a sign. "So early?"

"I know."

Clarence told me if a woman plays with her hair when she's talking to you that means she wants you. He also said we point our belly buttons to those we trust. He learned that on CSI. Majorly sad, Valentina was doing neither. "So how come you have to leave?"

"Ah, it's silly."

"Well, how come you have to leave, you? You should just stay. We're going to the Park tomorrow. Maybe we'll do the snake ceremony and the Bison Creep."

"The what?"

I decided to just go for it. "Those were the ceremonies I used to do in your name."

"Holy," she turned and was facing me. "Tell me more."

"Ho ho! Got your interest now, hey? Well seeing as how you're all cheap and taking off, I might as well confess my night moves to you."

"I have to hear this."

"I'll tell you, but you have to tell me who's waiting for you down south."

"Ah!" she laughed. "Look at you. On the keemooch, hey?"

"Well, maybe I'm not so sneaky after all."

"It's not a He, if that's what you're thinking. It's a She."

"Oh?"

"Ho ho! Look at you. You wish I loved women."

"No, I..."

"It's for my girl."

I sat up. "You have a daughter? I never—"

"No. It's for my car."

"You're leaving for your car?"

"Do not ever buy a convertible."

"How come?"

"Because if you bust the back window, they have to sew it back in."

"Hunh. And they have to do it tomorrow?"

"Yup. Tomorrow. I have to meet them at the shop in Edmonton."

"How cheap. You're not even gonna see what I used to do for you."

"Well just tell me."

"Wait. How did you break the back window?"

"It's a long story."

"A long story, she says. Maybe your legs were just high, I guess!"

She laughed a throaty laugh and her head went straight back. It was a laugh so beautiful and loud. But it was manly in a way. Manly in a good and sexy way.

She looked directly at me. "So tell me about these ceremonies held in my honour."

I took a big breath. "Which one do you want to hear?"

"The snake."

I nodded. "Okay, so you know how I used to be in Senior Naturalists?"

"You were?"

"Yeah, it was the best. We had so many field trips. So we used to do this thing when we wanted someone, we used to sneak away from the camp and we used to go into the caves."

"Oh they stink," she wrinkled her nose.

"Like hot apple juice," I said, registering it was eerie the way that she knew.

"Go on," she said. Maybe she caught me thinking. Maybe she could sense thoughts.

"Well, we had this ceremony where we would chant the name of the one we wanted and we would roll up our sleeves. You had to do this when the snakes were mating. There were hundreds of them all balled up."

"Eee!" she said and wiggled. I could see the little girl in her the way she laughed, the little girl my grandpa saw.

"So you had to roll up your sleeve and put your hand through a ball of rolling snakes. If you could go all the way in without getting peed on, that meant she'd fall in love with you."

"And you said my name the whole time?"

I nodded. "Three times." I could still remember all those snake eyes watching me. It was weird. In the dreams I had for a month after, I was back in the cave on one knee with my arm wrapped in snakes. All those garter snakes were hissing and asking me, "Areyousureareyousureareyousure?" as something stood and walked closer behind me. I got scared and shivered.

"What?"

"Oh I got scared just now. I got the heebees."

"Ah you. Tell me the other ceremony."

"Oh. The Buffalo Creep." I started to get cold and wished I had my jacket. It was at the coat check, past Gunner. This wasn't so fun anymore.

"Come on. Don't hold back. This could be your lucky night."

With that, we both started laughing. Out of shock. Out of delight. Out of lonely. I'd love to hold her tonight. Those hips. Those long legs. I wanted her to smother me with her body and warm my soul.

"Hello?" She snapped her fingers. "Tell me the ceremony. Sing it to me."

I looked at her. *"Sing it to you?"* Maybe my grandpa was right. Some spirits free you only if you sing to them. "Well," I said. "We also used to go to the Bison Creep on the fourth of July."

"I remember that. Only boys were allowed to go."

I nodded. *Yup.* This was when Uncle Raymond was bringing back the Indian Way to town. He wanted everyone to learn Cree, Dene, or Slavey. He invited all the non-Native kids and their families to learn, too. We had four awesome summers of Back to the Land trips, and we even had Winter Camp, where families of all backgrounds got to work together living a traditional life. Clarence has pictures and keeps saying he'll make copies. My favourite picture is me, Brutus and him with our cowlicks and big horse teeth smiling away as we hold up the rabbits we caught in our snares. At the same time—it was funny—I didn't want him to make copies. I loved that I had to go to his house and bug him to dig it out and show it to me. Brutus liked it, too. I could tell. His eyes would shine when he remembered us as kids with all that life ahead of us.

"How come you guys lived so far out of town?"

"It was my dad," she said. "He didn't like people."

Hmm. I thought. Or maybe he was protecting Smith from you.

She looked at me and her eyes flashed.

I panicked and spoke quick. "Last time I seen you... you were with Greg." I knew her husband before he passed.

"And you were with what's her name—Lisa?"

I winced. *The Bog Monster.* Lisa. I aged forty years just remembering her name. "Yup. We've come a long way, hey?"

"Yup."

"So you wanna know something magic?" I asked.

"What?"

"Years ago. I'm talking years. I was at the dump."

"Mm. Hmm."

"I found a diary."

"Oh?"

"Yup. It was half on fire. I saved it."

"Was it mine?"

"No. It was Justin's."

"No way."

"Yeah."

"Who would have burnt it?"

"Maybe his mom?"

"Maybe. It was on fire."

"Take it easy. How do you know it was his?"

"He signed his entries. It was his handwriting."

"Yes, but how do you know it was his?"

"We were in school together for every year until grade nine."

"Oh. Sorry."

"No, it's okay. He had a few letters he'd sent to you when you went out."

"What?"

"Yeah."

"What did you do with them?"

"I burnt them. Sorry."

"Did you read them?"

Why lie to a spirit? "Actually... yes. I won't lie."

"Oh God."

"No. They were sweet."

"Mine or his?"

"Both."

"What grade was this?"

"They were actually when you were both in university."

"Oh yeah. The long distance. That must have been '93?"

"Maybe."

"Okay, so what did you see?"

"I just saw a lot of love and respect and hope."

"Yeah. I had a lot of hope for us."

"I miss him."

"Everyone says that, but did you ever really know him?"

"I know that he liked to streak."

"Yes. He did like to streak. But did you ever sit down with him or share time with him?"

"... No... I guess not."

"Do you remember him ever making eye contact with you?"

"... No ..."

"Yes. That was Justin. A ghost to his own life."

I wanted to touch her hand. "Sorry. I don't mean to bring this up to hurt you. I just wanted to come clean."

"Oh now. There's worse things. I wish you would have saved those letters. I would have liked to read them again."

"Well I did save something."

"You did?"

"Yup. The thing is I got robbed a while ago." This town was getting bad for break-ins.

"No way."

"Yeah way."

"Where were you?"

"House party. It was cheap. I crashed out at this party and when I woke up my glasses and wallet were gone."

"Were you drinking?"

"No. That's the thing. I just fell asleep and whoever it was came into my room."

"Oh that's creepy."

"I know. It really got to me."

"So what did you lose?"

"It was an excerpt from a letter to you."

"A poem? He was always writing me poems."

"Yeah. Kind of. It was more like he was thanking you."

"Me? For what?"

"For a summer he'd never forget."

"Ha ha! You're kidding."

"No. I'm not."

She looked concerned. "Did he make any specific references?"

"Well, not exactly. He said thank you for not judging him. He wrote, 'Take me back to the place where there are no words' over and over."

"Oh. OH! I know what he's talking about."

She looked away. She was blushing.

"Well?"

"Well what?"

"You're blushing."

"So?"

"So what was the thing he was thanking you for?"

"Oh now. Do we really want to go there?"

"Why not? You can just tell me. I've been wanting to ask for, like, twenty years. Maybe more."

"Oh. Maybe more, huh?" She smiled.

This was fun. "Yeah."

"Holy! Here we are at our reunion and here I am getting raked over the coals, boy."

"No. It's not about judgment. It's more about awe."

"What?"

"Oh come on. We went out in grade nine."

"Ha ha. For like three days?"

"Still."

"Still what?"

"We have a history."

"There was that one night."

"Yup. We almost got to second base."

"Ha ha! You wish!"

"I do," I nodded. "I really do."

"We didn't even come close."

"Yeah. Why not?"

"Well, remember I asked to see your chest."

"Oh yeah. And I was like: I'M NOT INTO MUSCLES, BABY. I'M INTO VEINS!"

"Ha ha and you whipped off your shirt and you were trying to Bruce Lee out."

"Ha ha. Yeah. I was seeing stars I was flexing so hard for you."

"I remember. In fact, when I close my eyes I can still see you."

"I blew it that night, hey?"

"Yup. You blew it."

"Sorry about that. You know, that was the first time..."

"What?"

"That was the first time I ever encountered what turns women on."

"What do you mean?"

"Well, you grow up and you're trained, you knew? We're all trained to look for a 36-24-36."

"Jeezus! Who is that?"

"You?"

"You wish!"

"Actually, no," I said. "I think you're gorgeous. I won't lie. I think you're perfect. But that night you told me what you wanted."

"I'm a sucker for a great chest."

"Yeah. Sorry I was just nuts and ribs. I think I had worms back then."

"Ew."

"Ha ha."

"Gross. Don't talk about it!"

"Sorry. I was really skinny."

"Yup. You were. But now..."

"I've been working out."

"I see that. I hear you guys are still streaking."

"Yeah. Every couple of weeks."

"That's great."

"So... I want to know what he was thanking you for."

"Why?" She asked.

"Because I think I've known you for your whole life. We're, what, mid-life now? We grew up together and we were close, you know? And now everyone has these adult lives, kids, old ladies, homes."

"And?"

"I just wanted to be welcomed into a place like that. Where there are no words."

She put her hand on mine. "I am sorry for what happened."

"Me too," I said. "It's been tough." But then I realized: what were we talking about?

"Wait," I said. "What are we—?"

"He wasn't thanking me for anything I did. Not really."

"What was he thanking you for?"

"Ah. I can't say."

"Oh come on."

"Please. Look. You're blushing. Remember how moose meat would always make you blush."

"Yes."

"Well, just tell me."

"What? What does moose meat making me blush have to do with anything?"

"I was just fishing."

"Fishing? For what?"

"It's a technique."

"A what?"

"It's a technique for getting info. You give a little to get a whole lot more."

"Ah geez."

"Justin taught me that."

"When?"

"His first summer back from law school."

"Where did he teach you this?"

"At the lake."

"That was his favourite place, hey?"

"It used to be."

"Okay okay. So what was he thanking you for?"

"Can't say."

"Come on. I double Dogrib Dare you to share it."

"Hey, you can't use that!"

"Why not?"

"Because you know I never back down."

"Nope. You never did, so why stop now?"

"Look. I can't talk about it and you've cornered me. Is that where you want me?"

A spirit cornered. "Maybe."

"Grant, you've had a rough year. A horrible... I can't imagine it. I don't want to imagine it. I've thought about you this past year. I wondered how you were."

"Thanks."

"Justin and I had this thing he'd like to do. All I... Ha ha. Oh God. You're getting me to tell you."

"I'm just curious. I'm allowed to be curious. We're mammals, remember?"

"What?"

"So you were saying."

"I can't talk about it."

"Why?"

"Because I feel like I'd be betraying his trust."

"Can you show me?"

"Ho-lay! You're just bold, hey?"

"Well who's on a plane in nine hours?"

"Eight. What does that have to do with anything?"

"That's your get out of jail free card."

"Wha! You want me to show you what we did?"

"Yes," I dry swallowed. This was my chance. I couldn't let her back on that plane without trying. "Yes, I do. Just show me. Take me to a place where there are no words."

"Hmmm."

"Hmmm?"

"Hmmm. Okay, you tell me a secret and I'll consider it."

"Okay," I said. "Do you have any ideas how many times I wanted to get on my mountain bike and ride out to your house and sing to you?"

"Take it easy."

"I'm serious."

"Okay. What song?"

I threw back my head and laughed. 'We are the World.'"

"What?"

"Remember—with Bruce Springsteen? Man, I practised it for you and everything."

"Was Boy George in that, too?"

"I can't remember. I think it was 'Tears are Not Enough'."

She started laughing. "This is awesome."

"Okay," I said. "Let me go back in time and learn that. If I knew you liked 'Tears are Not Enough' more than 'We are the World' I would have learned that for you."

"Wait. You know what song I really loved?"

"Tell me."

"'Feed the World.'"

"Oh yeah! "Feed the woooorld. Don't they know it's Christmas time at all?"

"Yeah!" we yelled.

"I tell you," I said. "I would have stood there air humping and singing to you if that would have gotten you out of your home for a kiss."

"Ho ho! That's a classic right there." And then she leveled her eyes at me. "So where can we do this?"

"We could go back to my house."

"And you're not going to tell Clarence or Brutus?"

"Nope. I swear. Just you and me."

"You won't judge me after?"

"Well, I don't know what it is."

"Swear it."

She was being serious. "I swear it."

"What are you swearing?"

"I'm swearing that I won't judge you after."

"But will you judge yourself?"

"Wait," I said. "What?"

"You may be surprised at what it does to you after."

"Take it easy."

"I'm serious. You will suffer."

"Come on," I said.

"Ha ha. Okay, you will suffer deliciously."

"Oh my."

"Yup. Oh my. Oh my."

"So do we need anything?"

"No. Just a shower before."

"Hey hey. Now we're talking."

"Grant, if we do this... you know we can't go back."

"... I know."

"You know if I show you this, you'll never... I don't know... You'll never think of me the same."

"I don't think of anyone the same anymore."

"I know..."

"So you really want to do this?"

"I do."

"Everyone's watching us talk. Especially Gunner."

"Yup. They've been watching us all night." She focused on me. "So how will I go to your house?"

"Leave when you want and meet me there."

"You kept it?"

"Yup."

"Number 14, right?"

"Yes."

"What time shall we meet?"

"Twenty minutes?"

"I'm ready to go right now."

"I'll warn you once..."

"What?"

"Justin cracked a molar it got so good."

"Holy!"

"It's true. Got a good dentist?"

"Who cares? I'm Treaty!"

"Ha ha. Me too!"

"Ha ha!"

"Ha ha."

"Okay, so I'll go to the trailer but I won't turn the porch light on. Just let yourself in."

"Okay."

"I'll leave in a bit. Don't drive. Everyone will see your car."

"Grant."

"Yeah?"

"I think you think I do something, but the truth is it's all you."

"What?"

"It's something special, but you have to do it. I just show you how."

"Whoah. And it'll change me?"

"Forever."

I thought about it. "I could use something special."

"Then it's yours."

"Wow."

"Okay, I'm leaving and I'll see you soon."

"Put fresh sheets on the bed and light a candle. What I say goes. You're not allowed to talk."

"Okay."

"You have to do everything I say."

"Okay."

"I won't stay the night."

"Okay."

"I'll leave when we're done."

"Okay."

"You can't call me after."

"Why?"

"Because I decide when and if I want to do it again."

"Wow."

"I've never done this with anyone else since Justin"

I almost believed her. "Okay."

"I'll only do it with you and you have to swear you can't tell anyone."

"I swear."

"Swear it on your mother's memory."

"I swear it on my mother's memory."

"Okay. Talk is cheap. I hope you're ready."

"I'm ready." The music started up and it was loud. "More and More and More" came on and it was one of my favourites, but it was way too loud.

"And shave."

"I already shaved today."

"So shave again. Use a new razor. Baby soft, okay?"

"Okay."

"Okay. I'll see you there."

"No. You'll see someone like me."

"What?" This scared me.

"When I see you next, your name isn't Grant anymore."

"Okay. What is it?"

"I'm going to ghost you."

"What?"

"Because you reached through snakes for me."

The music got louder. "Wait. I didn't hear—"

"And because you sang my name to the buffalo people."

"Wait. I want to understand—"

"Tell me what Gunner has threatened you with."

"What?"

"He and his brothers are waiting for you to leave. I can tell."

I looked down. "I'll be okay."

"No you won't," she said. "They've come for something."

I swallowed hard and closed my eyes. Maybe she was the one. Maybe it was all true. The one who was here to protect us all. "He said he'd break my legs if I testified against him."

"When?"

"Tonight. If I came to the reunion."

"So why would you come if you knew this would happen?"

I looked into her eyes. "Because I knew you'd be here. I know you're the one who sings the snow. I've seen you in pictures back at the Treaty 11 signing. Also, with my ehtsi. You're timeless and I'm so scared. I don't want my legs broken."

She touched my hand and looked in the direction of Gunner and I saw her eyes flash with something. "You go first. Because you've invited me in, give me an hour. I'll be at your house when I'm ready, and I will be hungry."

My blood turned to slush.

"Prepare a dish for me. Your very finest. You've called me now. We'll feast and then I will devour you."

I was suddenly more scared than ever.

She looked to them like a wolf who sniffs the weak in the wind. "Now go. If you hear something behind you when you walk out, don't look back. Promise me?"

I nodded. I was so scared. "Okay."

"Promise me."

I swallowed hard. "I promise."

"You're safe now."

She gave my arm a gentle squeeze and, for a second, I felt like a rabbit with a wolf's jaw around it, squeezing.

I thought of their mothers. "What are you going to do to them? Gunner's mother is sick—"

"Go," she said. "They may find themselves with their legs sewn on backwards tomorrow, or they may find themselves as your new protectors. I'll offer them a choice."

"Why?" I asked. "Why are you really doing this for me?"

Her eyes darkened. "Because I'm sworn to you. In the future. You're part of something that needs to happen. Tonight they would have broken your spine and your short ribs, and we would have lost everything."

The skin on the left side of my body lifted and I shivered. My teeth started to chatter.

"Go now," she said. "Don't look back."

I nodded. "Got it."

And I went. Without my jacket. Without meeting anyone's eyes. And I didn't look back when I thought I heard the screaming, the whimpering, the begging. As I hit the four-way, I ran all the way home.

Blood Rides the Wind

"Just so you know," Rob looked at me in the rearview mirror, "we weren't really expecting anyone for a week."

I was quiet but nodded. I could smell smoke on me, the smoke from burning the last of my grandmother's clothes. Rob's sleeves slid up, and I caught a glimpse of a tattoo. *A claw? Teeth?*

"Oh now," Sue looked back and glanced quickly at my lip as she ran her hand up Rob's arm. "Don't you worry, Bear. Rob could use a lot of help while I'm away."

I nodded and looked away. The trees were so much bigger here in Simmer than in Rae. Spruce and pine. It was like we were being hugged from far away. As the plane landed, I saw pelicans flying. Forty of them all circling the town together. I didn't see them the last time I was here. They were ever neat. As we pulled up to the residence, there was a student with two hockey bags smoking outside.

"What's he doing back here?" Sue asked.

"Dean's not supposed to be here," Rob said with a low voice.

"Rob," Sue said. I could hear concern in her voice.

Right away, I did not like whoever this Dean was. He had a scowl on him. Typical northern scruff: baseball cap, Tap Out hoodie, jeans, running shoes, smoker, goatee. He was trying to grow a mustache and he was short. He worked out, wore a black Affliction short sleeve, but it was his eyes that I didn't like. They were mean.

He nodded at Rob and Sue. "Hey," he gleeked snuff by his shoe. "I'm back."

Rob spoke to him from the Suburban. "I thought we agreed this program wasn't for you."

"Yeah well," the young man said, eyeing me. "My dad says different and he'll send thirty grand if I come this year." He spat again. "I'm hungry. Feed me."

Rob looked at Sue while he slowly got out of the Suburban. "Honey, why don't you get Bear set up and I'll get to the bottom of this." He limped towards Dean. Rob had a bad leg. I wondered why he didn't just use a cane.

She looked tired and let out a long breath. "Sure. Bear, let's get your things and find you a room."

I nodded. All I had was my backpack, my weapons bag and my poster carrier.

The first thing I saw when I walked out of the Suburban was a sign that read: "Our family supports a drug free home. If any drugs are found in our home, we will call the RCMP. We support youth learning in a safe and drug and alcohol free environment."

"Who's the harelip?" the young guy asked.

I looked at him fiercely. "Now, Dean," Rob said. "Is that respectful? This is Bear from Behchoko."

He spat towards me. "A Dogrib with a retard name." He turned to Rob. "How's the knee?"

Rob placed himself between Dean and me. "Let's go upstairs. You know where the kitchen is."

"Girls still get the basement, right?" Dean said. "Sweet."

Dean turned to me and gave me a dirty look. I looked away. Rob and Dean walked upstairs towards where the kitchen must be. Dean had left his bags in the middle of the door. Sue moved them and sighed. "Do you need help, Bear?" she asked.

I shook my head. "Who is that?"

She sighed. "Well, between you and me, that's Dean Meddows. He was asked to leave last year... I'm surprised he's back. His dad is the chief and we could sure use the money, but I would not be surprised if Rob asks him to stay elsewhere. He's trouble."

"Thank you for letting me stay," I said. "Sorry for mixing up the dates."

She looked at me and I could see tears well up. "Oh now... I'm just glad we were here. Usually, this time of year we're still down south, but you know... it's actually great timing. I have to leave tomorrow."

Sue was a good person. She had kind eyes. "Is everything okay?"

"It's my dad. He's not doing so well." She looked in the direction of where Rob and Dean would be. "You go pick your room. There's a key in every lock so once you pick your room, keep your key with you, okay?"

"Do you have the newspaper?" I asked.

She stopped. "Oh. Good question. I'm sure we do. It's around here somewhere. I think we have it in our suite. I'll leave it in the kitchen for you. Are you hungry?"

I shrugged.

"Well, why don't you let Rob sort Dean out and help yourself when you head up," Sue said. "Go pick out your room.

You get first dibs. Oh. Can you keep an eye on our dog Duke? He's really sick."

"Sure." I trust dogs. "What's wrong with him?"

"He's just not eating."

"Was he poisoned?" I ask.

"What?" She looked at me. "No. Why would you say that?"

I shrugged. "Usually, when dogs are poisoned they don't eat."

She frowned. "Can you remind Rob to take Duke to the vet tomorrow? Our appointment's at three."

"Okay."

She sighed. "Okay, I'm off to call my brother. Our suite is here and you can knock on our door anytime, okay?"

I nodded and went to find my room.

I looked in every room and decided on the one at the end of the hall to the right. It had a view of the field and I could sneak out if I wanted. It had its own private sink and mirror as well as a small study desk and closet. The bed was small but the room was perfect. It had a wall of cork board so you could put up posters and there were tacks of many colours just waiting to be put to work. I locked the door and started putting up my Bruce Lee posters and started unpacking my UFC and WWE DVDs. Would Rob cook for me? What if he wanted to eat with me and talk? I only ever ate with Ehtsi and Wendy and we always ate in silence.

I had a week to accomplish what I came here to do. This was my base and I knew the town a bit. I'd been here last year for my grade eleven but stayed in a basement apartment where they didn't ask any questions. I could not tell Marvin I was back. He'd want to hang, but the principal was staying somewhere in town. I'd find him and he'd never walk again. I swore it to Wendy before I left. I went through the mental photos I'd taken of the residence and stored in glances: there were crosses in the hallways. Were they Catholic, Protestant, Anglican? No ashtrays. A few cigarette butts. This was a drug-free home. I counted a shoe rack capable of holding twenty pairs of shoes. There were photos along the hall of northern students who'd stayed in the residence for the past decade as they attended PWS. It looked like in winter they went on a caribou hunt. In the summer, they probably went to check nets and make dry fish. Everyone looked so happy. In each of the photos, there stood Sue and Rob beaming with pride. I wondered if they had kids of their own. I'd read the paper and find out about the trial and the lawyer's arguments. Maybe the local paper would have different news from CBC and News/North—

Dean Meddows opened my door and threw his hockey bags on the floor. "Hey, ugly. Get out of my room." Up close, he was way shorter than me. He still had his baby teeth. They were coated in plaque and they looked like yellow toenails.

How did he—? I'd locked that door. I knew I locked that door. He was serious.

"Are you deaf? Get out of my room." He started looking around. "Nice belt," he said and started looping it through the rungs in his jeans. It had been on my dresser right next to my tote bag. He then reached into my tote bag and pulled out my nunchucks, throwing stars and Ehtsi's knife. "You a frickin' psycho, or what? I'm keeping all of this or I'm telling on you."

"Get out of here," I said. He had small arms and that meant a small reach.

Dean scowled at me and tapped my belt. "What are you gonna do—fight me?"

I tucked my chin and dropped my hands to my sides, Bruce Lee style. He saw this. "I'm not asking you again. Get out of my room, harelip."

I made two fists and stared at him. "Put everything back and get out of my room."

He turned to me and smiled. "Oh good. Ugly wants to fight. I'm keeping the belt and weapons."

I pretended to be scared by backing up. "Don't—"

Dean put his little fists up and grinned. "I got two sledge-hammers here and they're called 'Good' and 'Night.'"

I shook my head.

He scowled at me. "God, you're ugly."

I sized him up: I was taller and had a longer reach, and I bet I knew his trigger. "At least I'm no midget."

He put everything down. Dean's eyes bugged in his skull and he turned purple with anger. Bingo. With that he pulled his arm all the way back and started running towards me, telegraphing his move. I let him come, drinking in the air and savouring what was about to happen. I spun against the image of where I thought he'd be and, like a windmill, I back-fisted his temple—Crack!—with all I had. He crumpled to the ground. He smoked his forehead off of the floor. I winced at the sound. His back started shaking and he gave a few little kicks.

I watched to make sure he wasn't faking. I pulled my belt off him. *"I am ugly,"* I thought and licked my top lip, *"but I'll always be taller than you."*

Blood flowed from his nose. His eyes rolled in his skull and he had spit down his face. He blinked and looked around. "Wha—?" He curled his wrists into him and looked around, blinking. "Holy... you... knocked me out..." I was quiet and watched him in case he wanted to fight again. He curled his hands into cups. He touched his nose with his thumb and looked around.

I couldn't let him get up.

I rolled him so he was face down. I then straddled his back and pulled both of his arms up over my legs. "Hey. What?"

I then sat down on his back and heard the gristle in his back-strap snap, crackle and pop. He started wiggling with all of his might to get away, so I leaned back as I began wrenching on his jaw with my fingers braided under his throat. This way he couldn't scream. I had him in the Camel Clutch. "Tell me about the boy who called Social Services on the principal."

"NNNNggggh," he grunted. His little hands were quivering he was in so much pain.

I lifted my weight off of him a bit so he could speak. "I won't ask again." I lowered my weight on his spine and heard sinew pop some more. I saw his hands turning purple. He started kicking and shaking terribly. "NNnnnggggh!!"

"Talk," I said as I sat up a bit. I felt something warm seep down my fingers? Spit? I lifted myself up a bit so he could talk.

"Gerald," he gasped. "Everyone knows it was Gerald."

"Last name," I sat back down and heard another pop in his lower back but eased up enough so he could talk.

"Spruce. You're giving me the Camel Clutch?"

"Stay out of my way and live." I hissed into his left ear. "Get in my way again and I'll blind you." I pushed him off of me and stood. Right away he turtled up and started grasping for breath. I glanced at my fingers. Blood from others can make you sick. It was tears. He'd been crying. I spun around and pulled him out of my room by my belt and his collar down the hallway. I reclaimed my belt. "You sucker-punched the wrong person," he wheezed. "You wait and see." I grabbed his legs and dragged him to the room farthest from mine. He didn't resist. I grabbed his two stink hockey bags and dragged them out beside him before closing and locking my door. I repacked my weapons bag and continued setting up my room. *What if this got me kicked out of here? Ah. He'd never tell, the big coward.*

Once I was all set up, I examined and retried my lock with my key. It locked, so how did Dean get into my room? Maybe I hadn't locked it. I'd tell Rob. I had to fortify my room. I looked down the hall and Dean had chosen a room to the left. I paused and listened. It was quiet. I shook my head and made my way into the kitchen. Rob was sipping a coffee, looking out over the yard. The moon was out. It was about a third full. The last time I was here, I made a friend: Marvin. He'd talked me out of maiming the principal the first time; I should have never listened to him.

"You all set up?" Rob called.

I nodded. He looked nervous. His meeting with Dean must have been a disaster. My knuckle started to burn.

"See Dean?"

I eyed the coffee. It smelled great. I nodded.

"I'm not sure what to say about Dean but lock your doors and windows while he's here. I'm working on getting him gone as soon as I can, okay?"

I looked at my fingers. "Do you change the locks here every year?"

"What's that?"

"Someone can use their key from last year to get into my room."

"I wouldn't worry about that. Once the students are gone, they usually ask for the same room again. The last student who used that room came from Smith. He graduated."

"I don't trust my lock," I said.

He was quiet. "Okay, well, maybe that can be one of your chores tomorrow. You can change your own lock with any of the others you wish. How does that sound?"

I nodded and stood there, unsure of what to do. Did he serve me coffee, or did I serve myself? That's when I noticed he had an ice pack on his knee, under the table.

He turned the ice pack over and pointed with his lips towards the coffee maker. "Help yourself."

I did. Lots of whitener, lots of sugar. Where was the paper? I had to read the paper to get the latest on the trial.

"I bet you're hungry."

I nodded. The back of my hand stung from striking Dean's temple but I felt great, not even winded.

He got up and limped to the oven. There were beans and perogies. His knee. *Why had Dean asked about his knee?* Rob opened the stove door and there was a plate wrapped in tinfoil. His sleeves rolled up again and I saw that he was tattooed on both arms. His tattoos were faded but still looked cool—the face of Japanese demons. "Ketchup's in the fridge."

I was too shy to go get it. I didn't want him watching me. I grabbed a fork and knife and sat at his side so we could look out the big window together. I pulled my hoodie up and started to eat.

"You were here last year, hey?" he asked. "How was the other residence?"

"Good," I nodded and could feel him wanting to ask me more but I turned away from him. I wanted to eat but started to get shy again.

"So this year," he said, "we'll be looking for captains to help us lead the caribou hunt. Have you ever hunted caribou before?"

I shook my head. My drunk uncles kept saying they'd take me but they never did.

"Well, maybe this is your year to learn how," he said and he said it so gently, like it was a wish that he held for me.

I looked at him. "That would be awesome."

Rob stood slowly, keeping his weight off his knee. "I'll leave you to your meal. Please wash your own dishes when you're done, okay? I gotta go check on Duke."

"Thank you," I said. "Do you have the paper?"

"Yeah," he said. "It's by the phone." He pointed to a table filled with books. "Bear, I'm glad you're here. Sue's dad is sick. Her brother's been watching him but he's got to get back to work. I'll need help cutting wood and doing the grass. And changing your lock."

I nodded. "We can't forget to bring Duke in tomorrow at three." I had a feeling someone poisoned him.

"Okay," he said. "We'll talk in the morning. Welcome to your new home." He stopped and looked at me. "Is there a reason you showed up a week early?"

I had a feeling this was it: the moment that would decide if he'd let me stay, so I decided to tell the truth. Most of it. "I can't go back," I said suddenly, surprising myself.

"Where? Rae?"

I traced my finger over a scratch in the table. I decided to go for sympathy. "Our Grandma passed away last week."

And there it was: the truth. She was gone. All the promise and everything of our family. Dead with a nest of lies in her heart from my mouth. The lies I told her. I felt my ribs tighten with this. "Thank you for giving me a home. I can work hard."

He nodded. "You are welcome. I'm sorry about your Grandma."

I pulled my hoodie back so I could look down and not be watched. "I hope Sue's dad is okay."

"Me too," he sighed. "Hey, we've got the TV set up with satellite downstairs. We've got a Playstation, Xbox 360, plenty of games, a small library. It's all downstairs. The students sound-proofed it last year for that Dance Dance Revolution, so have a good night. We'll have a nice breakfast tomorrow, okay? We have a week to get the residence ready for the students."

I nodded as he left for his and Sue's room. "I'll help you," I lied.

I pulled my hoodie back and ate everything on my plate. All the while, I listened for Dean. He better not be messing with my room. I downed a cup of coffee and I found some cookies. Raisin. My favourite. With fudge? Whoah. I ate them quick. They were ever sweet. I watched the golden moon in the sky, and I said a prayer for Wendy, for Sue and Rob, for Sue's dad and their dog. I had made it. I had arrived to do what I had to do. It was August 22nd. The moon seemed closer than in Edzo or Behchoko or maybe even Yellowknife. She was beautiful.

I was now ready to read the paper. I moved to the table and sat down. There it was: front page. It was all true. The principal was going to gct off because the methods used to retrieve the server on his hard drive were illegal. He had a lawyer who did all the talking in the article. There was a picture of the principal. It said his sentencing date would be on September 8ᵗʰ, the first day of school. There was no mention of Wendy. All it said was "allegations of indecent exposure." There were no pictures or mention of his wife, who I would love to interrogate. But that was after Gerald. I had Gerald Spruce's name and, with the phone book, I quickly had his number and his address. At the front of the NWT phone book, there's a map of every community in the western arctic. I could see how I'd get to his house: go left facing the river, take a right on Ptarmigan, follow Loon Street until it becomes Slave River Narrows Avenue and then walk a ways to Sky Crescent. I'd start at the beginning and work my way up.

I tidied up, turned the coffee maker off, did dishes. There was no way I was going to blow this. As I walked back to my room, I passed by Dean's door. I listened: no sound at all.

I knelt and checked my door lock. It looked fine. I gripped it and turned. It stuck. *How did he get into my room?*

I unlocked the door and listened after I closed it. Nothing. Still no movement from Dean. Everything looked exactly the same as I left it but I didn't trust any of this. I hid my weapons bag under the bed—way at the back. I tucked only my Grandpa's sheathed bone knife in the small of my back behind my belt and jeans. I wouldn't need my nunchucks or modified throwing stars. I turned out the lights and jumped out of my window into the cool night of one of the last days of summer. I'd keep it unlocked so I could get back in later. Because we were north, it would get dark at around ten. I couldn't wait. I had to meet the boy who called Social Services. As far as I could tell, he was an ally. He tried to protect Wendy. He'd taken the stand at the trial. I'd find out what happened and what went wrong.

I could not run into Marvin. Couldn't. He'd try again to talk me out of what I had to do. I followed the map in my head and looked around. Fort Simmer was a pretty town. I looked at the moon. "I miss you, Ehtsi." I swallowed hard. "I miss you, Wendy."

There was nobody out. A few dogs barked. There were some nice log houses. Everybody here, it seemed, mowed their lawns. I looked into windows: lots of TVs and computer screens. There was one house with a lot of trucks on the lawn. Through the living room window, I could see into the kitchen: a card game was in full effect. Everyone had hunting caps on, maybe to hide their eyes, and soon I was outside Gerald's. His family had a nice log house with a large workshed out back. There were two trucks out front: a nice Ford and a beater, probably for the bush.

I could circle round and watch through the windows, but he was an ally. I had to remember he was an ally. I had to work fast and gather my own information. I took a big breath and looked up and, to my amazement, I saw a fleet of ten, eleven, twelve pelicans soaring miles above, like white hands blessing anything below. Not once did they flap their wings. They soared and veered together as one. I wondered what Wendy thought of them when she was here, and I wondered what they thought of her.

"Can I help you?" a voice called.

I folded my tobacco bag and looked up. Shoot! My hoodie had blocked my view. It was a man holding a chainsaw and a long file. He'd come out of the shed and must have seen me.

"Hi," I said. "Is Gerald Spruce here?"

"Inside." He waved and went back to work behind the house.

I nodded. He didn't suspect a thing.

"Gerald!" he called.

"What?" a voice called from a back window.

"Company."

"Who?"

"Looks like an Indian: skinny—straight nuts and ribs."

"What?" two voices asked: one from the back window and one from the kitchen window. They must have been open with the screens on.

I could hear someone walking and I readied myself. I dropped my hoodie and used both hands to smooth over my hair.

A woman with an apron that read "Hot Stuff" and moccasins answered the door. "Hello."

I nodded. "Hi. Is, uh, Gerald here?"

She studied my lip. "Son? There's a young man here to see you." She looked to me. "Come in. Please."

So much for sneaking up on anyone. *What kind of ninja was I?*

I walked in and she held out her hand. I nodded and took it. She stared right at my lip again before making eye contact. "I'm Gerald's mom. And you are?"

"Bear."

"Wow. Quite the name. My son's just out of the shower. He'll be right out. Can I get you some tea? Coffee? Take your jacket?"

I shook my head. She'd see my knife. "Tea would be nice." I could smell sweet pine and spruce in the wood box directly in front of me and there were pictures of a young man everywhere. This must be Gerald. To my surprise, there was a yellow fireman's helmet on top of the coat rack and a large set of flashlights.

"Well come on in," she said.

I stepped out of my shoes and walked into one of the most incredible log houses I had ever seen, maybe the only actual log house I'd ever been in. There were wolf hides, bear hides, a few stuffed foxes on the top floor looking over. There was a gun rack filled with hunting rifles and everything was so clean. There was a small couch around the biggest wood stove and there were plants everywhere. You could smell them. Green. Fresh. It's like their breath pushed against everything in the room. I bet you could load that wood stove and it would burn all night. There was also a nice supper table and a sewing machine was set up. There was dough dust on the counter and a large silver mixing bowl had a tea towel covering it. Cookies were cooling on racks and my mouth started to water. There were two huge green Tupperware bowls beside one another by the coffee maker. "You arrived just in time," she said. "Cookies'll be ready in five minutes."

I nodded. It smelled delicious and sweet.

"I got tea here. It's fresh. How do you like it?"

"Two and two," I said. "Please."

She motioned for me to sit down at the table.

I glanced quickly and tried to memorize everything about this house. "This is the most beautiful home I've ever seen."

"Well, thank you." She poured my tea and came my way. She was carrying cream in a can but no sugar and no spoon. I glanced at her moccasins. Yup. They were exactly like what Grandma used to wear. "I don't believe I've seen you here before, Bear—is it?"

I shook my head. Of all her things, Ehtsi's moccasins were the last to go up in flames. "I'm here with the Northern Leadership program."

"Oh," she said and leaned back to look at the calendar on the wall. "School doesn't start for a week."

I went to reach for the cream but looked around. There really was no spoon and no sugar. "I'm helping Rob. Sue's dad is pretty sick."

"Oh?" she asked. "He's got Alzheimer's, hey?"

I poured my cream in and looked around for a spoon. "I didn't know that." I'd trade information to buy time and build trust. "Her brother has to get back to work so she's flying out tomorrow. Do you have any sugar?"

She nodded. "Well, Robert needs help. After what Torchy and Sfen did to him, he's lucky he can walk."

I looked up. I'd met them before when Marvin and I were smoking up on the high school roof. I played dumb. "Who are Torchy and Sfen?"

She shook her head. "Two of the nastiest boys you'll ever meet. Brothers. We lock our doors now because of them."

The front door opened and the man with the chainsaw walked in. He looked at me and nodded. He had woodchips all over his cap and hair.

"Stanley," Gerald's mom called, "if you get any wood on my floor, you'll be sleeping on the couch tonight."

The man looked at my lip, frowned and looked back at his wife. "Baby, I did my best to brush myself off. I even took my coveralls off."

She narrowed her eyes. "You forgot your hair."

"What?"

She made a rolling motion with her fingers. "Brush off your hair."

"Jay-sus," he said. He nodded at me, looked at my lip and went back outside.

Norma huffed. "Anyhow, what was I saying?"

I held up my cup and craned my neck to follow the vines that ran along the loft above us. "Do you have sugar and a spoon?"

"Oh yeah, Torchy and Sfen." She shook her head. "He'll never walk the same way again."

I held my tea. It smelled good. "What happened?"

"Well, the way I heard it..."

The bedroom door that had been closed now opened. Out walked a young man who looked seventeen, like me, who had the biggest mullet I had ever seen. It looked like he fluffed it up on purpose. Two big rolling balls of hair rested on each shoulder. He stopped, looked at my lip and looked at his mom.

"Gerald, this is Bear."

"Hi." Gerald looked back at my lip while I looked at his hair in complete astonishment. He looked like Elvis with his hair like that. Then his dad opened the door again and came in without any shavings in his hair. His cap was off and he had Hat Head.

"Okay," his dad said. "Let's try that again."

"Sorry," Gerald said. "What's your name?"

Everyone was looking at my lip. I held up my hand. "I need sugar and a spoon."

"Oh for goodness sakes," Norma said. "Sorry. Gerald this is Bear. Hun, this is Bear. Where are you from?"

"Behchoko." I said.

"Rae or Edzo?" the man asked.

"Rae."

He nodded.

"You're Wendy's cousin," Gerald said.

My face flushed and the room became still.

"Oh God," Norma covered her mouth. "Oh God. I'm so sorry."

I nodded.

"Norma, get the boy a spoon and some sugar." He came around the corner and he held out his hand. I stood and shook it. It was a bone-crushing grip and he nodded at me. He was handsome. I liked him right away. After that, Gerald came forward. I could smell cologne. They had the same nose, but Gerald had a purple hickey on the side of his neck.

"Mom," Gerald said, "maybe we should all have tea."

"Did you just get in today?" his dad asked.

I nodded. I heard a squawk and realized there was a hand-held walkie-talkie plugged into a charger on top of the fridge.

"He's here to help Rob. Sue's dad's getting worse."

"He's got Alzheimer's, hey?" Gerald's dad said. He looked at his son. "Sorry about your cousin, Bear." I froze. "My son here's the one who called Social Services on him. You guys want cookies, or what?"

We both nodded.

"Are you going to the Walk for the Cure?" Gerald asked.

I looked at everyone. "What?"

Gerald's dad and mom got us all tea, sugar, spoons and cream properly. Tea was poured and a huge plate of fresh cookies placed in front of us.

Stanley spoke. "It's a fundraiser. For cancer. The whole town shows up and you walk all night. We're all doing it.

Every year we beat Yellowknife, Fort Smith, Hay River for funds raised."

I took a big breath and realized I was exhausted. "I didn't know about it."

"You don't know about it? It's in the paper, on the radio. We have to outdo Yellowknife this year, no matter what."

"You look like you need a good night's sleep," Norma said.

I nodded. The tightness in my chest was there but it had loosened since walking into this house and just sitting. It had been a tough week: burying my grandmother, reading the paper to see the principal was going to get off, hitching a ride to Fort Simmer.

"What do you want to know?" Gerald asked.

I looked at him and suddenly felt safe. I suddenly felt like crying. I looked at my hands. They were filthy. The smoke of Grandma's clothes was all over me and I could smell her. I could. I still had Dean's tears on my hands and ketchup from the perogies. I felt stupid for bringing my bone knife into this house. "How did you know?" I asked.

Gerald's mom touched her hair and his Dad looked down. There were no enemies here. Nobody reached for the cookies. Gerald closed his eyes and looked winded. He leaned back and let a long breath out. He looked to be in sadness. He then rubbed his chin and leaned forward and took a sip of his tea. "I can't believe they're going to let the principal off for what he did." He then stopped and looked at me. So did his mom and dad. I heard something. I was grinding my molars. I stopped. "Sorry, go on."

All of them went for the cookies and so did I, but I stopped when I saw my hands. I needed to wash my hands. If I was going to put anything in my mouth using my fingers, I had to wash my hands. But first I had to hear this.

"Can I just say something?" Gerald's dad said. "I think it's B.S.—excuse my French—that my son—"

"Our son," Norma corrected him.

"Sorry, babe. *Our son*. I think it's B.S. that our son had to take the stand and tell the truth when we all knew that molester was going to get off."

"That's not certain," she corrected.

"Oh it's certain," Stanley said. "The word's out: he'll walk. He's got nothing but money and lawyers."

I sipped my tea. So it was true. The paper said it might be true that the principal would get off because the RCMP messed up when they searched the house. "When do they reach their verdict or whatever?"

"The judge is flying up this week," Gerald nodded. With each nod, his hair bobbed. This was the biggest mullet I had ever seen. I thought for a second it was a wig, but, no, it was real.

I took a big breath. "Okay. So, how did you know?"

He nodded and took another sip of his tea. "It was the track meet. We were all there. Your cousin was very pretty. We didn't know she was deaf at first. She turned a lot of... heads when she came up but we knew she was different, you know, like... delayed?"

I nodded and thumbed my tea cup handle. I let out a sigh of grief and felt tears well up. "Go on."

"Well," he took a big breath and stopped. His mother reached out and rubbed his arm. "She, uh, dropped her, uh, pants and panties and started to, well," he took a hard swallow without his tea. "She began to masturbate in front of the whole school."

His mother cleared her throat and touched the back of her hair. It must have been long once. I closed my eyes and put my tea down. *Why, Wendy? Why?*

"You know what got him?" Gerald's dad said. "You know what got him? That little bastard was a cheapo."

Gerald stared at his tea.

"What?" I asked.

Stanley held out his hands and started counting off his fingers. "There's three kinds of Internet accounts you can get here: there's the one we have, which hardly uses any bandwidth or whatever, and then there's the usual one most folks use and then there's the corporate account or whatever and that's for business. You can download all you want. Mr. Principal was using the cheapo account and kept using up the town bandwidth. They had a summer student who couldn't figure out why the town server kept crashing, and it was because of what the principal was downloading. This kid has a peek and sees kiddie porn this and kiddie porn that and he called the cops. They had a look and went racing over the same day Gerald called Social Services."

"So how did you know?" I asked Gerald.

He let out a huge breath and was flushed in the cheeks. "Mom and Dad, cover your ears please."

To my surprise, they did. My eyes bugged when I seen his mom and dad cover their ears like little kids and look down. *What kind of family was this?*

He cupped his hands around his mouth, almost like to call a moose. "Her toes were painted a bright red and her you-know-what was... she was, well, she had been trained. I'm sorry to say it, but he trained her to do that... like that. The thing is, though, even before that, I knew he was wrong. I didn't like him as soon as I saw him and that's never happened before. I secretly called him 'The Devil.'"

I thought of Wendy: how the sunlight caught her hair. To see her, you'd never know she couldn't hear or that she was like a baby, but she was so trusting, always so trusting. And that smile. She was always—I buried my head in my hands and let out a huge cry. I started to cry so hard my body shook and I gasped for air. Snot and tears mixed as I cried into my ketch-up and I bawled and bawled and bawled. I felt hands upon my shoulders, rubbing my arms. The hood of my hoodie covered my hair and I gave thanks that it also muffled my cries. I was uglier when I cried. I thought of Wendy, how I used to train her for martial arts, how I did my best to prepare her for the world. I remember how the bear root only showed itself to her and Ehtsi. I remembered Wendy's sweet, trusting smile and me writing the letter to get her out of town. "Where's Wendy?" Ehtsi kept asking on her death bed. "On her way," I kept lying. "She's on her way."

"Bear," Norma said. "We're sorry. We're so so sorry. Don't you have a home?"

I shook my head. "Our Grandma died last week. We burned her stuff a few days ago." I took a big breath and wiped my eyes. My nose was running. I stood and made my way to the bathroom. I shut the door behind me and turned off the lights. I took my hoodie off and wrapped my bone knife inside of it. I washed my hands and face slowly. The soap smelled like berries from the city: fake. I was so tired. My body felt old. I cupped my face and squeezed. How could I? How could I have trusted anyone to look after her? I never should have written that letter. I should have known it was too good to be true. I let out a long breath and wiped myself off. How embarrassing. I blew my nose and shook my head. It was too hot in the house. I squeezed my hoodie hard and felt the bone knife in the middle. I slowly opened the door and they were all sitting, looking down. I made my way to the chair and sat down. "Sorry," I said. I put my jacket on the table beside me.

Norma reached out and patted my arm. "You're hurting and you need support. Don't you have any family?"

I shook my head. "Not anymore."

"What about your cousin?" Gerald asked.

I thought about it. "She's with the nurses now." They had a group home for developmentally delayed kids and teens. She was there. The last time I went to see her, she turned her back on me and ran to the corner and started crying.

I wiped my eyes thinking about her and the promises I made to check up on her when we were both here last year. All broken.

"Bear," Gerald said, "there's something. We don't know for sure if the principal will get off for the kiddie porn and for what he did to your cousin, but they will get him for stealing the money he stole from the kids."

"Money?" I asked. I helped myself to a chocolate chip cookie and it was delicious. Gerald's dad sat down with a fresh cup and moved my old one away. He poured me a fresh cup and put two scoops of sugar and a lot of cream. "I know how Dogribs like their tea: double-double, hey?"

I nodded and looked for Kleenex. I sipped and it was perfect. Nobody was looking at my lip anymore. "Thank you," I said to everyone in the room. "What's this about money?"

Gerald nodded. "The junior highs start fundraising as soon as they start grade eight to go to Disneyland in grade twelve as part of their graduation. We didn't know that all that money was being kept by the principal. We gave it to him assuming he was putting it in the bank for us, but he was keeping it."

"What a jackass," Gerald's dad said.

I looked at Gerald and his huge hair. "So they may get him for theft?"

Gerald nodded and took a bit out of his cookie. "They say he took thousands and blew it all when he and his wife took off."

"Why would his wife go with him if she knew he was doing all of that?" I asked.

"There's rumours," Gerald's dad said, "that she didn't have a choice. She's saying he forced her."

"She turned him in," Norma said and nodded.

I scratched my head. Without my hoodie on, my scalp started to itch. I had another cookie and sip of tea. It was perfect, and I felt lighter. Somehow, I felt lighter. I'd been tight in the chest, like I couldn't fill my lungs the past week.

Norma spoke softly. "She called the cops from a gas station and told them which way they were heading for BC."

"They used a spike belt on the car," Gerald's dad said. "No one's supposed to know that, but it's true. I would have loved to have seen that."

I nodded. "So he blew all that money?"

Gerald scratched his neck. "They say he's using it for his lawyers now."

"So why are you here?" Norma asked.

"What?"

"Why are you here? If your grandmother passed away— and we are so sorry to hear that—if your cousin is in Rae, why are you here?"

I cleared my throat. Should I tell them? Should I say I've come to paralyze the principal and blind him? That right beside me is the knife I aim to use?

Just then the front door opened with a quick knock. In walked a young woman who had lipstick on and smiled when she saw Gerald. Gerald stood and walked to her. "Hey, babe."

"Hi," she said as she walked into the house, putting her purse on the bench by the porch. *What a pretty girl,* I thought. Her hair was still wet and she wore glasses that showed off her dark eyes. She was short and she looked at Gerald's folks before she looked at me and my lip. "Hello."

"Baby, this is Bear. He's Wendy's cousin."

"Oh," she said and raised her hand to her lip. She walked towards me and I could smell bleach from her. "Hi. I'm Donna." She shook my hand lightly, once. I caught a blurred hickey across her neck, under her ear. Classic.

"Do you want some tea?" Norma asked her.

"No," she said. "I left the truck running. I'm late."

Gerald looked at her and then at me. "Bear, we've got to go. We're MCing the third hour for the Walk for the Cure. You're welcome to join us. We're all going. The whole town shows up. It's basically one big party, except you walk all night and visit."

I shook my head. "I've got to get back. Rob needs my help first thing."

"Sweetie," Stanley looked to Norma, "why don't you go with the lovebirds and I'll drive Bear back."

I stood. "I'm okay."

He held his hand up. "I insist."

Norma nodded and walked to the closet. "Gerald, can you get those cookies? They're all ready—with your shoes off please."

Gerald walked across the room and grabbed two huge Tupperware bowls filled with cookies that I had missed completely. This was why the house smelled so good.

"So," Donna said, "how big is that Bingo tomorrow night?"

Norma pulled out a light jacket. She walked over and gave Donna a huge hug. "The jackpot is five grand."

"I have a good feeling," Donna nodded. "We've got water bottles in the truck, right?"

"Yup," Gerald's dad said. "Your folks there?"

"Already walkin'."

"Wow," Stanley said. "I'll be right along."

I caught Norma giving Stanley a look, like, *What are you up to?*

He puckered his lips really quick and smiled. They had their own sign language.

"Okay," Donna said and looked at me. "It was nice meeting you. Welcome to Fort Simmer." She looked at Gerald. "We have to go. What grade are you in?"

"Twelve," I answered.

"Us too." She rolled her eyes. "I can't believe school starts next week."

I nodded. She was actually beautiful.

Gerald walked to me and held out his hand. "It's good to meet you. If you want to talk, call me: 2888. We'll be there for the sentencing. We'll see you, okay?"

Norma came and gave me a big hug. "You come here anytime you want a good supper. They say your problems never seem so big after a good meal."

I nodded. "Thanks."

She kissed her husband and patted his bum. "No hockey. Come walk."

"Ho. Not even," he smiled at her. "I'm going to drive Bear around. Show him the town."

With that, Norma, Gerald and Donna made their way out of the house and I was left alone with Stanley. He started clearing the cups and plates. "Want some more tea?"

I shook my head. "I'm good."

"Take some cookies with you," he said.

I shook my head.

"Come on," he said. "Don't be cheap to yourself. Rob would probably like some."

I nodded. "Okay."

He handed me a Tupperware. "Fill that skinny little bannock leg of yours."

There was a pile of cookies. I could bring some to Sue before she left.

"You never answered Norma's question," he said as he put the dishes in the sink.

I knew what was coming. "Which one?"

"What are you doing here?"

I looked at my hands. It seemed stupid now. I'd come here to cripple the principal. I didn't know where he was. I was a lousy ninja. Was the principal in jail? Did he sleep in his house? Was he at a hotel? I'd read that his house had been seized.

"School," I said.

"You're in grade twelve, right?"

I nodded.

"You came here last year, right?"

I nodded. *Shit.*

"Well, welcome back," he came and sat down. "You'll graduate with my boy."

Our boy, I could hear Norma correct him.

"You two can help lead the caribou hunt."

I winced and he caught that.

"So if you're here coming to school, what's with the knife?"

I was stunned. *How did he? How did he know?*

He pointed to the bathroom. "It was poking out when you went to the bathroom."

I blushed.

"I know why you're here, Bear. I can see it in your eyes. You want revenge. I've been smelling blood in the wind for the past week and now you're here." My face was on fire. He sat back and eyed me. "That's pretty arrogant of you, don't you think?"

I glared at him. "What do you mean?"

He fanned his hands out and made them move like the wind across the table. "The Great Spirit moves in many different ways. Don't you think the man upstairs has a plan already set in motion for the principal?"

I shrugged. This was basically the same stupid speech Marvin gave me.

He leaned forward. "Are you really going to throw your life away when the best is yet to come for you?"

I shrugged again. Tears started to well up again.

"I'm sorry about your grandma and your cousin. You're too young to be carrying a load like that, but I'll tell you what. My son—our son—we're so proud of Gerald. I seen you checking out his hair."

I smirked. His hair was huge. "He looks like Elvis."

He grinned and took a bit out of a cookie. "Well, you know why he's growing his hair like The King? He and his best friend Jonathan made a pact in grade seven that when they graduated from grade twelve they'd have mullets as they walked across the stage for their diplomas. They wanted the whole town to laugh at them. Then they're going to donate their hair for cancer research. Wigs... for people fighting the big C."

I looked at him quickly. His eyes were so caring. "That's my boy." He stopped and considered something before he spoke softly. "I read your letter, Bear."

I looked down and swallowed hard.

"I'm on that committee, too."

I shot up and went for my jacket. "I have to go."

"No!" his voice boomed and I froze. "You'll sit and you will listen to me. You brought a knife into my house around my wife and son. Sit and listen."

He meant it. My body went weak with fear. I sat back down and looked at my hands. I wanted to vanish.

"It's not your fault, Bear," Stanley said calmly. "You wanted your cousin to hear and speak. You wrote that letter out of love. I was the one who approved it. Sue seconded it." Sue? My heart froze. She must know why I'm here.

"I got a copy of it in the next room. All the committees and boards I'm on, that was the one that touched me. You and I and the rest of the board had no idea what would happen." He took a big breath. "No one. We all trusted the principal and his wife." He touched my hands with his once, softly. "Bear, listen to me." He held his hand up and showed me his watch. It was big and beautiful: polished silver with a face that had many cool dials on it. He then took it off and placed it in my hand. "I'm going to make you a trade." He patted my hand. "Put it on."

I'd never owned a watch before. The watch's bracelet was silver and the face—or dial—was beautiful. It had a moon on it with three small circles: one for the day, one for the month, one for the date. I could feel it ticking. "Whoah."

"This is the last watch my father ever gave me. I was in grade twelve when he did. Try it on." He then stood and made his way to a small room by the fridge. I fumbled with the watch and folded the bracelet. I thumbed it shut and it clicked. It fit. It was heavy and huge, but it fit.

Stanley came back holding two boxes. They were wooden. "Put it on your left hand."

"Oh," I said. I couldn't find the clasp. He sat down next to me and put the boxes to his right. "Na."

That was Dogrib. I looked at him and he smiled. "Bet you didn't know we were related, hey?"

I beamed. "How?"

He put the watch on my left wrist and clasped it shut. "Your grandmother was Melanie."

I nodded.

"I met her once. Very powerful and gentle. A midwife."

I nodded and teared up. He was making me miss her.

"Bear, you are now wearing a Citizen Chronosphere. You can't get these in Canada. My dad was a watch fanatic. Those little circles in the dial are called complications. That little doo-hickey is called your moon phase dial."

I looked at it. "Are you giving this to me?"

He shook his head. "I'm trading it for your knife."

I looked at my jacket. "I can't. That was the only thing of my Grandpa's that I kept."

"Hear me out. Remember I talked about Gerald's best buddy Jonathan?"

I nodded.

"Ever since my son called Social Services to investigate the principal, the town has turned his back on him. Thank God for Donna. We were worried about Gerald. Last year was tough on us. All of us. Jonathan never spoke to Gerald again. For some reason, people here turn their backs on people who call the cops or Social Services, even when it means they save lives or protect children." He then pushed two boxes towards me and opened each one. They were two of the most beautiful watches I'd ever seen. "These are Citizen Campanolas. You also can't buy these in Canada. I bought two: one for Gerald and one for Jonathan. This was months ago, before it all happened—and I saw the crime scene."

I looked at him and realized I could not know anything more about what Wendy had been put through. I know she needed stitches after. I closed steel doors around any more emotion or images and totally focused on these watches. They were big with designs I'd never seen more and they had sun faces in the dials. "Here's your deal, my man. I want you to reconsider your quest for revenge."

I glanced at my hoodie where my family knife was.

"I want you to focus on your schooling. I want you to come over here whenever you want. Heck, we'll feed you any time you want. I want you to be a friend to Gerald. He's never known any of his Dogrib cousins. You get your grade twelve and when you walk across your stage you can have one of these watches and return my dad's watch to me. I will then return your knife to you."

My jaw dropped. "Why?"

He took a big breath. "Because you deserve your own family. You deserve a house filled with memories and laughter and great cookin'. You deserve to hunt for the people and cut wood for those who can't cut it themselves and know the pride of serving your community. You deserve to see the world. They say the best revenge is living a good life." His voice then lowered. "Don't get in the way of the Creator's plans for the principal. Always remember, the Great Spirit moves in mysterious ways."

He had tears in his eyes when he spoke. "Trade your family knife for the last watch my dad ever gave me, Bear. I trust you with it. I can tell you're a good person." I glanced again at my jacket. I then looked at the two watches in front of me.

"Get your grade twelve. Then go on to college or university and return home and help the people. Have you ever hunted caribou before?"

I shook my head.

"Neither has my boy. You two can learn together."

I needed to blow my nose. "That would be nice."

"Have you ever made dry fish?"

I shook my head. Gerald's dad handed me a box of Kleenex and I grabbed a bunch and looked away to honk my nose.

"What you're feeling now will pass," he said. "I promise. What the world has in store for child molesters is not kind. Wait. You'll see." He tapped my hand and touched his father's watch. "Think about it." He rose and showed me the watches one more time before gently closing the lids. "I'll drive you home." He walked back to the room where he'd gone to get the watches. I didn't know where to put the used Kleenex, so I tucked it into my sleeve just like my Ehtsi used to.

I suddenly realized I had the most beautiful watch around my wrist and something like a wish inside of me. I marvelled at the watch, the weight of it, the spell it cast. I felt giddy. I tapped the Tupperware filled with cookies and rose to get my jacket. There was Grandpa's bone knife in its sheath. I handed it to Gerald's father as his father's watch hung wonderfully from my wrist. He placed it on the table and pulled the blade from the sheath and whistled. It was razor sharp and jagged at the same time. I'd sharpened it on the stove coils back home. "This ain't no killin' knife," he said with a low voice.

I put my jacket on. "What?"

He slowly ran the blade across his thumbnail before turning it over and running his thumb over the blade. "Knives with grooves near the spine are called 'blood gutted' blades. It's so the muscles can't grab the blade after you stab someone. You can just keep stabbing. If a knife isn't blood gutted, well, you get one punch with it." He put the blade away and tapped it gently.

I nodded and looked again at my watch. *Who was this man?*

"Looks good on you," he got up and took the walkie-talkie from the top of the fridge. It beeped when it came off its charger. "We'll take my truck."

"I'll walk," I said.

"I need you to do something for me," he said as he grabbed his jacket.

I frowned.

"Come on. Don't cheap out on me now."

He pointed with his lips to a small ledge by the porch. "Grab those cards for me."

I looked. There was a deck of cards still shrink-wrapped sitting there. I took them. He put on his runners and so did I. He pulled on a dark jacket that read Coroner on the back. He also grabbed a DPW vest, the kind they use for Highways work.

I handed the deck to him and he put it in his inside jacket pocket. He then picked up a tiny remote that looked like a car starter and clicked it. Music suddenly rose through speakers all over the house. It was a sweeping chorus of voices. It felt like praying and it was like something you'd hear at mass or at Christmastime.

"It's Enya," he said as he locked the door behind him. "The plants love it."

We got into his fancy truck and he started it up. "There's a subclause in our trade: I'm going to ask you to do one thing but you must never, ever tell Norma or Gerald."

I looked at him. The cookies were still warm in the Tupperware. "What?"

He backed out of the driveway. "Man to man," he said. "I need your word you won't tell."

"Well, what is it first?"

He raised his hands. "*Ischa*! Where is the trust?"

I nodded. I couldn't tell if he was being serious. I didn't know what to say.

He looked at me with the biggest smile. "Nephew, I need you to set the clock on my truck." I looked to the dashboard. The clock read 10:39. "Ever since that frickin' Daylight Savings Time, that sucker's been off an hour and it drives me crazy. Every day when Norma and Gerald ride with me, I gotta hear..."

There were many buttons: some for the radio, some for the CD player. I looked at my watch: 9:39. It was getting dusky out. I pressed down on "Clock" for a few seconds while he talked and the time started flashing. I turned the knob on the left to the right and the ten started flashing. I went right but that made it eleven so I turned it left and that made it nine.

"So," he said. "I'd be eternally grateful if you—"

"Done," I said.

He stomped on the brakes. "What?"

"All done," I said, pleased with myself. I hadn't smiled in a month and there I was: grinning, amazed.

"Holy shee-it," he said. "You did it."

I nodded.

"How the heck? Nephew, you are a miracle." He reached over and messed up my hair. I flinched but then let him. I wasn't used to anyone touching me. He pushed me gently. "Holy Moses," he said. "Do you know how many frickin' hours I have spent trying to solve this mystery?"

I beamed as he drove me down a new street. As we made our way together, I could see the moon. I held my watch up. Stanley had set it so the face on my watch was the exact shape of the moon in the sky. "That watch is solar powered. You'll never need a battery."

"Take it easy," I said.

"It's called an Eco Drive."

I looked at the moon above the trees.

"Now lookee here. Our annual Walk for the Cure." There were at least one hundred people walking on the track. On the sides of the track, there were tents and a few small fires. People were walking and laughing. There were kids. Around the track, on the inside lane, there were small lanterns with candles glowing inside.

And there was Marvin, my buddy, walking with his mom. It was so great to see him. I bet he'd love the cookies I had. He'd lost weight and he was smiling. To think he'd been a bully to me when I first met him.

Stanley continued. "We got a lot of cancer here. Gerald never knew his grandparents. There's something about this town. Maybe it's the Tar Sands. Maybe it's the uranium they used to make the bombs."

I looked at him. "What?"

He nodded. "The uranium used to make the bombs that were dropped on the Japanese came from up here."

"No way," I said.

"Yes, sir. Rayrock Mines and Port Radium. They transported it right through town. They're still finding rocks of uranium in people's gardens."

He shook his head.

I watched the people walk together. A few had flashlights. "Tonight, I'm going to walk with half the town: friends, my family. You sure you don't want to join us?"

I shook my head. I was tired. Tired and full. Maybe I'd call Marvin tomorrow.

"Okay," he said. "I'll drop you off and head back. Have you seen the renovations to the school yet? They put solar panels on it and a heat conversion wall."

"Nice."

He came to a four-way stop. "Let me show you."

It was a beautiful night. Dusk was settling in. No stars. No pelicans. Not a cloud. I could smell the spruce and pine.

"Let me give you your official welcome back. Fort Simmer is still population 2,500. Our town is still mostly Dene, Cree, French and English. They say we're the third-best place in the world to see the northern lights, but that's for marketing purposes. If you say you're third, no one ever questions you where the first two are. Keep that under your hat. Right now, our town is being hit hard economically. Numbers at the college are at an all-time low. The thing about Simmer is she'll never boom and never bust. If you're okay with that, you'll do just fine. Our town used to be a trading post during the fur trade.

There was a time when you could get eleven hundred dollars for one lynx pelt. Those were the good old days. I'm on the Chamber of Commerce. Next time I see you, I'll give you a mug, okay? I'm on the Tourism committee."

I nodded. "You're on a lot of committees."

He nodded. "Mm hm. I'm also the fire chief..." He pointed to the walkie-talkie. "And

I'm the coroner."

The spruce and pine smelled sweet. I loved this watch. I loved the tight fit of the band.

And there it was: PWS High. It still had a red brick front and there were a few portables around it to the left. This would be the year I'd finally get to see inside them. "Four hundred kids grade seven through twelve go here. Your graduating class will be around thirty or forty. They say a school is the heart of the community. We already have a new principal for this year. A woman. Believe you me: that was no mistake."

I looked at him. "Were you on the hiring committee?"

"I was," he nodded. Across the street was the swimming pool. I loved that place. I was good at swimming. Underwater, nobody could see my face.

"Holy cow," he said again. "Bear, do you know what I just realized?"

"What?"

He looked at his hands. "I can't believe I didn't think of this before."

"What is it?"

He turned his truck off and ran his fingers through his hair and then touched his cheeks before he looked at me. "I know why you're here."

I looked at him. I could smell the cookies in the Tupperware. I saw a small picture of him and his family tucked in the dashboard. Gerald had normal hair back then.

"Holy fuckin' moley, it's all clear to me. How could I have missed this?"

"What?"

"Do you know about the dojo?"

"What?"

"Do you know that Rob used to be a sensei?"

I thought of Rob and his limp. "A sensei for what?"

"I don't know. Jujitsu or karate. Batman stuff. I hear they punch rocks."

I looked at him. "Wow."

He nodded. "He tried last year to tame Torchy and Sfen. We advised him against it but he went ahead anyway. How do I know this, you ask? I'm on the school board. He thought he could turn those two, but they turned on him once they got what they wanted. Not only did they shatter his knee for him, they stole a sword from him."

"Sword... what kind of sword?"

"Nephew," he started jumping up and down in his seat. He was like a little kid. "I come from a family of prophets. No lie. I can't believe I didn't see this before." He looked at me and beamed. "Oh man, oh man, oh man." He looked left and right like he just couldn't keep it to himself. "My boy, you are part of bigger plan. Never you mind the principal."

I shook my head. "But he's going to get away!" I said.

"Let's hit the pause button on that for now. But here's the deal: a long time ago, the museum board inherited a full suit of samurai armour and a real samurai sword. How do I know this? I'm on the board. Our museum inherited a real samurai sword and a samurai suit of armour by accident. It was a clerical error. We've been trying to return that armour and sword to Japan for years. Rob was the director of the museum a few years ago and kept the sword in his dojo. He was working on it, tracing the family history. It turns out it is an Emperor's sword, a sacred sword, but for some cheap reason, the Japanese government never got back to him. We don't know why, but the night Torchy and Sfen double-banked Rob, they destroyed his knee and stole that sword from him."

"How?" I asked. "Why?" But then I thought of something: "Duke," I said out loud. "I bet you any money that Torchy and Sfen poisoned Duke before they tore into Rob."

"What?" he asked.

"Duke," I said clearly. "Rob and Sue's dog is sick. I bet he was poisoned by Torchy and Sfen."

"Why would you think that?" he asked.

"I'd do it," I said. "If I knew I had to take out my sensei and he had a guard dog, it would be necessary."

"Holy shit," he said. "You're right."

I thought of my grandmother's medicine. To cure a dog who's been poisoned, you need sulfur and frozen meat.

I had an idea. "Do you have any sulfur?"

"Yeah," he said. "Why?"

"I need it to help Rob."

"You know what's crazy," he smiled. "I have some in the back. We were just harvesting some for the science camp. Take as much as you need."

I would help Rob by healing Duke.

"See?" he said. "It's all making sense. You're Dogrib. Those brothers are Dogrib. You're with Rob and Sue now. You're here to return the sword to Rob because he's always dreamt of returning the armour and the sword to Japan. That was his dream from the beginning." He turned to me. "Bear, I swear to you now as a man who has predicted things before, you are here to return the sword to Rob. He needs that sword. Torchy and Sfen are fighters. They're wicked. But you can do it. Get that frickin' sword back."

"How?"

He shrugged. "You're on a path. I can see it. Hell, I can smell it. You go to Rob. Learn the story but play Dumb Indian. Remember the rule in Simmer: even if you already know it, pretend you don't. Play Dumb Indian so you can learn even more of what you already know. Learn what happened in that fight. Do what you need to do to get that sword and that armour back to Japan, back to where Citizen watches are made. Man, don't you see? These watches, that sword—it's all a sign. You're no frickin' ninja. You're a hero in waiting. Hot damn, I'm good!"

He slapped his hands together and started shuffling in his seat and he started dog paddling the roof. "Okay, okay. Cool down. I gotta go to the Walk for the Cure. I'll drive you home."

"No," I said. "I'll walk. The residence is just over there, hey?" I pointed past the school.

"You're Indian," he said. "Point with your lips, you."

I got shy. My lips were ugly.

"Come on," he said.

I frowned.

"Don't give me your poopy lip."

I looked at him. "My what?"

"Here in this town, we raise our kids tough. When a kid's hurt, you know how their little bottom lip sticks out?"

"Yeah."

"Well, our job is to go and say, "Oh. What's that? A little poopy lip? A bird's going to land on your lip and poop on it. This way, Indians from here don't cry. Don't you know that?"

I shook my head and started laughing. "That's crazy."

"What's crazy is an Indian pointing with his cheap fingers. Now come on. Show me what you got. Where's your new home?"

I looked past the school and felt stupid but I did it. I pointed with my lip to the residence.

Gerald's dad pushed me. "Right on the money, nephew. You got it. A natural. Hot damn, this is a great night. Okay, walk and have fun. We're in the book. Come by anytime. Your family knife is safe with me. I shall return it with your Campanola on the night you and my son graduate, okay?"

I nodded. "Okay."

As he drove, Stanley pointed with his lips to a house that was burned down. "Torchy and Sfen." He drove a little further and pointed to a duplex. One of the sides was totally obliterated by fire and smoke damage. "Torchy and Sfen."

"What?"

"They torched over thirty houses in one night starting with the principal's." He shook his head. "That was the longest night of my life." He let out his breath. "Fuckin' fire bugs."

"Wait," I said as we passed another carcass of a house. "They burned down all these houses?"

He nodded. "Funny thing, though. Each one is where the sexual molestation of a child took place."

I studied him. He was thinking something big and quiet. "So are they in jail?"

He sighed. "They're on the run."

Ninjas, I thought. "And you want me to go after these guys for a sword?"

"Sure," he said. "Like I said: you're Dogrib. They're Dogrib. Work something out." He looked at his father's watch on my wrist. "I'm worried about Rob. Do what you need to do to get that sword from Torchy and Sfen."

I had no idea how the heck I was going to do this, but I felt something. They'd taken ratroot from me that night we met. They were astonished by it. They respected its power. I could get more...

"What?" he asked. "My nephew isn't happy."

I looked at him. "The principal's going to get away. He's going to do it again. If I'm your nephew, Wendy is your niece. She needed seventeen stitches. Four nurses had to hold her down because she didn't understand what was happening." I started to cry. "And she was working on her words. What are the words for what happened?" Tears stated to cloud my eyes. "You're the coroner and on the board of of everything in this town, and you're going to let him walk? I'm sixteen. Do something!"

He thought about it. He was quiet for a long time.

"I didn't know about the stitches."

I wiped my tears away but even more were coming. "Don't you know everything?"

He let out a long breath. "I guess not."

He looked off. "There's one thing I've learned and I get the sense you should know this—and here's another reason you can't attack the principal."

"What?" I asked.

"The principal," he said, "had a partner."

"Who?"

"Someone in town. The cops have tried to catch him but he keeps vanishing. They've never seen anything like this."

I felt cold again. "So you're telling me that the principal had help, that maybe my cousin wasn't molested alone?"

He closed his eyes tightly and shivered. "Yes," he said. "The principal's wife has come forward and said he had a partner. Nobody but the cops and I know this."

I felt so cold, like someone had iced my soul.

"I'm sorry, Bear, but I promise you this. We will find whoever this is and we will punish them both. You dig?"

I nodded.

"This town used to be so perfect," he said as he gripped the wheel. "We used to visit, used to share. Now we have the hardest drugs and the same suffering they have down south."

I watched him. I could tell he wanted to say something. A secret maybe.

"Okay," he turned his truck back on. "Let's go for a ride." He put his truck in gear and we drove past the Elders' Home and the drugstore and the church. We then made our way to a large abandoned hospital. Part of it had sunk. Like a whole wing of the building. This hospital looked bigger than the new one.

"I'm going to let you in on something," he said and turned off his truck. "But you are not to tell anyone."

I looked at him and wiped my eyes. I hated myself for crying.

He put his hand on my shoulder and squeezed gently. "The first time I saw you standing in our driveway, I had this thought: 'That boy has so many tears inside of him.' And I hoped when I came into the house that I could take them away. Tonight, I think I can."

He thought before he spoke. "I spoke to a man once. He'd killed someone. He told me, 'Once you kill a man, you will never have a full night's sleep again. You'll live the rest of your life like a ghost.'"

My blood turned to slush. The way he spoke about my grandfather's knife not being a killing knife…

"Do you want to live like that?"

I shook my head. I suddenly wanted to go home.

"I am going to tell you a secret about this town. Every full moon when the men gather on the other side of this old hospital, we have a game called Furnace, though some call it The Running Man. What we do is we all draw from a deck of cards. Whoever gets the lowest card has an hour to run and hide in the hospital. Everybody pays to play this game. Even the runner. If they can hide for an hour or evade capture, they get the pot. If they can't, well, there's ten—sometimes twenty men with axe handles who are itchin' to find him."

I looked at the building. *Was he lying?*

"Tonight—oh in about twenty minutes, twenty or so men will be waiting to play under this almost-August full moon. Except tonight it's a Hunter's Moon. That means that tonight we already know who we're hunting." He looked directly at me. "We're hunting the principal."

"No…" I said.

He nodded. "Oh yes. I already know he's going to get off, and I won't stand for it. This is our town. I did not know about the stitches." He got very quiet. "So, my question to you is do you want to watch?"

He looked straight at me again, and I could not look him in the eye. I looked down. "Say the word and I'll show you how it's done. Or, I could drop you off at the residence and you could begin your school year and become my Tall Son. I would adopt you and you could become Gerald's best friend. This could be the greatest year of your life. You will learn to hunt moose, caribou, ducks. I could teach you how every moose carries a Bible. I could show you how the Dogribs honour our ancestors for Night of the Spirits. We could look in the bowls the next morning and maybe we'll see caribou hair to show us that great hunting is ahead for all of us. I'd love to come out to the fish camps the program goes out to year after year and see you and my son making dry fish together. Get that sword and suit of armour back to Japan. You're here for so many reasons and you're not alone anymore."

He looked at me again. "This could be your life. I promise you this could be a life with so much love on the way to you, or you could walk out—I would walk with you—and I would show you the women standing with their men, praying, as the men stretch, as the men ready themselves to hunt."

I looked at the moon and swallowed. My mouth was so dry. "What about Wendy?"

He nodded and handed me a water bottle from under his seat. I unscrewed the top and drank. It was delicious, freezing.

"Let me take care of her. I have a friend who owes me a favor at the Health Centre in Rae. She would take Wendy under her wing until you return for Christmas, spring break and when your grade twelve is finished."

I wanted to cry with relief. As long as she was okay. As long as she had someone. We were all we had left for family, but now I was being offered more.

"Wear my father's watch. When you harvest your first moose or caribou, I will give you your grandfather's knife back. Let that blade sing as we make dry meat together. I will show you how. I'll teach you everything I know for as long as I have you."

"Why?" I asked. "Why are you being so nice to me?"

"You are me forty years ago. I was angry, too. But I had a man I loved very much tell me that we always have to remember that there is man's way, there is God's way, and there is the Indian Way. And that set me free of so many things that could have ended the life that I deserved."

"So this game, this 'Running Man.' What way is that for him?"

He nodded and looked to the hospital. "Maybe all ways."

I drank again. I had asked a question I already knew the answer to. I felt free. I felt so excited for school to begin and for all the other students from across the Territories to come. I would help Rob. He would train me to fight. I would help him get the holy blade back from Torchy and Sfen. I swore it. I would get my grade twelve and I would learn all I could from Gerald's dad and his family. What would it be like to hunt caribou with kids my age? What would it be like to bring Wendy dryfish I'd made with my own hands?

"So," he said. "You get to choose: walk with me and see what's about to happen or go home and start over."

I nodded. All I wanted to do was go home, back to my room. All I really wanted to do was sleep. "Let's go."

This man who I suddenly fell in love with reached into his jacket pocket and pulled out a small pile of sewing beads. He put them in his other palm and showed them to me. "See these? I keep finding them all over our house. You know what they're for?"

I shook my head.

"My beautiful, gorgeous wife—who only gets sexier with time—is showing my son's girlfriend how to sew moccasins."

He poured them into my hand.

"That's my wish for you, my Tall Son. May the woman of your dreams teach the woman of your son's dreams how to make moccasins for him when he graduates from grade twelve."

He looked to my feet. "What's your size?"

I shrugged.

He smiled and started his truck. "You'll come for supper when things settle down, okay? We'll trace your feet out on some paper and get you a pair of moccasins for when you and your brother cross that stage together, okay?"

I nodded and closed my hand carefully around those beads. "Okay." I then put my hand on his. "Mahsi cho. Can I have that sulfur?"

"You may," he said.

I went to Duke who was lying down in the grass in his pen. He was so weak, he was panting.

"Duke," I said. "I'm a friend. You've been poisoned and I'm here to help you."

With what little life he had left, he started to whimper and growl.

I'd need meat. Caribou. To waken the wolf in him.

"What are you doing?" Rob asked. I never heard him coming, but I expected that.

"Sensei," I said as I turned to him. I held up the sulfur rock I'd been given. "Duke was poisoned by Torchy and Sfen before they took your knee and the sword you love."

He looked in wonder at me. "How do you know?"

"Did he faint and have seizures before they took your sword?" I asked.

"The day after. He was tested. We took him to the vet."

I shook my head. "They used mushrooms. Your vet would have missed this."

I could feel the energy change around him to anger. "How do you know this?"

"Before she passed, my ehtsi had dog medicine. I can cure Duke but I need your help."

"Anything." He knelt beside me and I looked. I saw only tenderness in his eyes.

"I need frozen caribou meat and a file and an ulu."

"Okay," he said. "Why?"

"We're going to slice frozen caribou meat into small pieces and pepper them with sulfur. Then you're going to stick the meat into the sides of Duke's mouth."

He swallowed hard as he looked at me and at Duke. "This is the only way to draw it out," I said. "It'll take all night. We can't stop once we start and we need to work together."

"Bear," he said, "if you save Duke, I promise you that I will train you in ways the world is forgetting. I will show you everything that Torchy and Sfen know, and then I'll show you how to beat both of them."

I thought about it. "Deal."

He took my shoulder gently and gave it a squeeze before he made his way back to the house.

I very carefully ran my hand through Duke's fur. "Duke, hold on. Your father and I are going to cure you and then we're going to get that sword. I promise you. I will be your father's greatest student. We are going to return that sword to its home."

I looked up at the stars. They were now waking from their great vanishing. I had a mission. I had a new contract. I would take on Torchy and Sfen and I would return that sword to Japan. Most of all, I'd return honour to myself and my family. I had to. For Wendy. For my grandparents. For me.

Tomorrow, if Duke was okay, I'd call Marvin. I'd tell him I was back. I was in grade twelve now and I didn't need to blow it. This, I decided, right damn then and there, was going to be the best year of my life.

Skull.Full.Of.Rust

This happened in a town everyone passes on the highway in Alberta. When you were a girl, you had a friend. We'll call him Tommy. You and Tommy had a secret game. You both called it "What am I thinking?"

It went like this: You thought very hard and very fast for a full minute. You wanted to think faster than Tommy could write because, after that minute, he'd hand you a sheet of paper with your thoughts printed out exactly on the page: *It's cold what's for lunch? I didn't do my homework did you? Can someone please turn down the frogs at night? They are so so loud. I wish the sun would come out and play.*

This was your game, and you could never win because Tommy wrote all your thoughts down. Every word. Exactly. This game always left you with a scent, a musk: a skull full of rust. You welcomed it. You felt ancient playing it until the day the stranger came to your school.

It went like this: you were playing alone when a man in a black suit wearing the shiniest shoes you've ever seen in your life approached you. He knew your name. He said, "Tell me where Tommy is."

He looked important. He wore dark glasses, ones you could not see behind. He smelled kind. A perfume blanketed you. A pretty smell. A pretty rust. When he smiled, you felt as if it were Friday at home time. You relaxed and suddenly remembered that Tommy was behind the school playing cards with the janitors.

Tommy had other games he could play with his gift. A few of the janitors knew that Tommy could bring luck, so they taught him how to play poker. Then they challenged men from town to come out to the school and play. Tommy would tilt his head and nudge the janitors into their next decisions about how to play their hands. The janitors never lost and were generous with Tommy and their winnings.

Tommy didn't come from a wealthy home, and Tommy liked what money could do. You thought about this as you led the stranger to the card game. He knelt down and whispered something into Tommy's ear. Tommy rose when the man stood. He followed the man to a car that was waiting on the school road. This car sped down the road and vanished and Tommy was never heard from again. The pretty rust the stranger left inside of you soured and stayed with you as you helped make sandwiches with your mother for the searchers, but you never told anyone the true secret of this, until you told this to me.

You've tried a million times to remember more of what the man looked like or how he asked to see Tommy but it's a mindblur, a ghost of a memory.

There, in the smallest room inside of you—under the rust—is where this story slept in quiet for decades. And this is where the party comes in.

Years later, after the guilt and mystery behind Tommy's disappearance began to fade, you were in art school. You were at a party. You were famous for how shy you were. Some thought you were a mute. Others thought you were eerie. "Don't Stop Believing" by Journey was just finishing and everyone was singing along when one of the louder men announced that he had just finished a workshop: "How to Hypnotize Anybody". The loud man in the kitchen got the crowd all worked up. They began looking for someone to hypnotize. Someone signalled you. Before you knew it, before you could stand, you were surrounded by people you didn't know who were chanting your name while this man fished out a silver stopwatch. Before you knew it, you were counting backwards with him as the only sounds you could hear were laughter from the hallway as other partiers had no idea what was about to happen.

And there it was again: you were filled with the aroma of rust. All of you.

You came to with a roar of people screaming into your ears to let go of the wall. You looked around and people were horrified. One woman was crying, looking away. Another was on the phone. Her cheeks were so red she looked slapped. There, in the corner, the hypnotizer was being yelled at by his girlfriend. She was pointing at you and yelling at him to "Help her!" You realize "help her" meant help you. They were all yelling at you to let go of the wall. You looked ahead and realized that the largest man at the party was hanging off of your arm, trying to break your stance. You looked at the wall and saw your palm and fingers had pushed through the wall and there was dust and paint chips on the webs of your fingers and on your shirt. Your arm and hand were throttling with exertion. You couldn't feel your hand, wrist or arm, until you heard a pop and the man fell to the ground when your arm gave. Immediately, your hand, wrist and arm tore in searing pain and you fell into the arms of someone behind you.

When you came to, the hypnotizer was on the phone with his teacher and they, together, summoned you "back to normal." All you remember was having the sensation of being catapulted from a field miles away back into your own body. Your arm felt snapped in half for a week. Ice and heat compresses and the occasional puff were the only thing that got you through. It was only later, after a dozen phone calls begging for him to "make it up to you," that you went to the hypnotizer's house where he and his girlfriend made you supper, that you understood the force you worked with.

"Who's Tommy?" the man asked.

"Why?" you winced as your arm throbbed with pain.

The idea, he explained, was to trick you into thinking you could hold up a falling wall and yell for help, yell for everyone to get out of the house as fast as they could—you could only hold it up for so long. The idea was to get everyone laughing at the quietest girl at the party who was now the loudest. It was supposed to be funny. Instead, you ran to the wall, planted both feet into the linoleum and slammed your palm through the wall. You see that when they remove the framed Van Gogh sunflower, there is your handprint embedded in the cement through the drywall. It is a perfect hand print in stone, pressed so hard that you can see the seven in your palm and the faint scar of a glass cut when you were a girl, so faint that you can only see it when you tan. "You started calling for Tommy to come home, to be with you and his family again," the man says looking down. "You were yelling you missed him. 'I've never forgotten you,' you kept saying. 'I'm sorry I gave you away!'"

Everyone was scared of you at the party because they couldn't break your grip.

"You were holding up the wall for Tommy," the girlfriend said. "And we couldn't help you. You kept yelling, 'How did the Devil know my name?'"

Years later, your flight was delayed. You were stranded with your portfolios of new work, work you couldn't believe that you'd done because it was of fire and horses and a lacerated field. These were the true faces of your dreams finally captured on canvas, and these were the faces of agony. This was the work of your life and you wouldn't hand it over to the airlines. You insisted on carrying your art portfolios onto the plane. It was because of the weight of your portfolios and the crush of the crowd that he ran into you.

He had changed, you said. He was an old man now, yet how could this be when you were supposed to be the same age? *Tommy.*

He was an old man now—sick in the blood with something inside him—and it was gnawing on him slowly and carefully. His lips curled when he told you to "watch it." He had so many missing teeth and the ones he had left, you said, would be better off pulled. He was almost bald. His skin was pasty, ashen, thin as paper. But his eyes hadn't changed. His eyes were still sharp, and it was those eyes that made you call his name: "Tommy!"

He wheeled around and took your arm, immobilizing you. "Who are you?" he hissed. All your weekend courses in self-defense, all the movies you'd ever seen that you stored in "what to do if" vanished and there you were, surrounded by hundreds of travellers, paralyzed. The strength of your legs. A cold shot through your body and you were dizzy, weak and that smell returned: a skull full of rust.

"I'll ask one more time," his foul breath—it reeked of cigarettes and hot pus. "Who sent you?"

You spoke your name, catching yourself to remember to not add your married name. He tilted his head to remember and eased the pressure off your arm and neck. He remembered you.

Without realizing it, you dropped your portfolios and were hugging him, calling his name. He was skin on bone, you said. It was like holding a bag of antlers. Here was Tommy. Finally...

"Where did you go?" you kept asking. "We thought you'd died."

"Shhhh," he hushed. "Tommy's not my name anymore. Hasn't been for years." He scanned the area around you, stopping once to look in your eyes and you grew dizzy, immediately dizzy. You remembered the police, the questions, the silence for years that came from the house he used to live in, his parents who never looked your way again.

"How much time do you have?" he asked.

"Hours," you lied.

"Buy me supper," he said, "and I'll tell you a story you'll never forget."

The man, Tommy said, that day, the stranger—was CIA. From the US government. He'd heard of a boy who could read minds and wanted very much to meet him.

After walking towards the car, they'd travelled for what seemed like days: the car ride, a train, two planes—very small and very fast—arriving at night, barracks, walking into a room full of children, and teens, all of whom could hear what others were thinking.

From then Tommy was trained in how to use his gift and play "What am I thinking?" to protect members of the US government and, yes, eventually the President of the United States.

"They called us 'Sniffers', but we called ourselves 'The Invisible.'"

He explained that when you see the President, you'll never see them. They are the ones who are selling ice cream, handing out flags, bumping into you and saying "Sorry—pardon me" in a goofy hat and ludicrous T-shirt, but, all the while, they're sniffing you, the crowd, opening strangers, tasting the currents, reading the air for delicate signals.

Tommy had been used in hostage negotiations, the ones that rarely make it to the news. He worked for the UN for several years, and became one of the President's closest.

You read, years later, that there were people who could leave their bodies and spy. There was a group of them from all over the world who wanted to see if they could visit the President. They slept and left their bodies from their homes to swim through the night skies to Washington. As they approached the White House, they were met midair by bodyguards who were doing the same, and were told if they tried to pass, they would be held in the air until their bodies died. In the distance, hundreds of bodies circled the White House: listening, watching.

"I was paid well for my gifts," Tommy told you. "I could have retired when I was in my thirties, but I stayed on."

"So what happened?" you asked. "Why are you so sick?"

"This?" he asked and pointed to his face. You realized then when you saw his yellow fingers that he was a chronic chain smoker, "This happened because the top brass—and I do mean the top brass—taught me how to erase someone with my mind."

He explained that if there was an enemy of the state, "the Sniffers" were trained to loop someone into insanity. The mind was much like a whirling soundtrack, he explained, but he could drive a thick, rusty nail through it. The CD would then skip like a broken record. Their targets couldn't get past one single thought, and that's all they would have for the rest of their lives.

"Is it a thought you plant?" you asked.

"No," he explained, "it would be the thought you were thinking last as I walked by and touched you. I got sick because I became the best. I could reloop or 'skip someone,' as we called it. I touched many people who were asking questions about the American government. People who were never the same again."

"After several years of this, I, too, began to question a few of the files. I was given less to go on after a while. Sometimes it would be a picture and an address. I'd ask why and I was told to 'just do it.' Some of them were mothers. I saw a boy once walking with my target. He saw me and waved. He smiled. And that was when I quit. He looked just like me when I was a kid. I couldn't do it. It was like the child of me waving at the man I'd become. Maybe it was the old part of me remembering my own vanishing, but I quit."

"Soon, I was ambushed. A unit of Erasers surrounded me and I looped myself. I declared myself insane, incapable of working another day. It happens. It's rare but it happens that someone like me burns out, but they had me in a warehouse for weeks and all I did was sputter, shit and piss myself, while I hid in the deepest part of me they couldn't read."

"I'd surface in milliseconds, once a month, until one month I peaked and there I was: in a sanitarium. It was a slice of Hell:

hundreds of people in a room all trying to get out. Hundreds of lost souls screaming. There was one guard I learned who was stealing from us and he was my target. It took me a day to escape and I've been running ever since."

"Where will you go?" you asked.

"I have a plan," he coughed, "and I'm going to live it."

He looked at the clock and motioned that he had to go.

"So who exactly were you working for in the CIA?" you asked.

"To this day," he said, "and this is the most terrifying part of all—is I don't think any of us will ever truly know. Maybe the Devil... I don't know."

You think he left you then with a hug, but you can't remember boarding your plane or going to your hotel or even ordering supper that evening or calling home.

You remember coming to, the next morning, with your right arm aching, reaching for the ceiling, and that smell of blood behind your face, gagged from your mouth, behind your nose.

All these years later and I think he "erased" you out of protection. He did, after all, suspect that he was being hunted.

When I thought about it, when you spoke about being hypnotized, your voice slowed, your eyes settled on your right hand. You put yourself into a trance speaking—so much so that my heart slowed with how calm your voice was. And I think this is the only way you remembered, because when I saw you, years later, I thanked you for a story I have never forgotten, and you had no recollection of your meeting with Tommy or with ever growing up with a boy your age with the gift of listening and hearing.

You had no idea what I was talking about.

And so, if you still don't believe that this story began with you, ask your husband about the comment you made on the phone that night, after you had found Tommy again. You said he asked you about it when you returned from your trip. He'd waited until the kids had gone to bed. He said you sounded so lost when you phoned, alone, but more than alone: lonely. He said before you hung up the phone, you said, "We are all creation, but some of us are monsters."

So, at your request, I've recreated the story you told me that day, in the airport, when our flights were delayed because you didn't believe me when I told this to you. And all of this is because I asked, "You know I am your biggest fan. I've always wanted to ask you, Why do you place such haunting red hand prints throughout all of your paintings? And you paint all those souls in agony. Forgive me for asking, but who or what are they reaching for?"

Because of What I Did

Crow pulls the rabbit inside out in front of us. Sinew snaps and pops. All that life and oh what little fur. No blood. She sets aside the lungs for Benny. They look like dragonfly wings soaked in water. She sets aside rabbit babies, and I close my eyes. Creator, I did not know she was pregnant when my hands took her. The babies look like toes. That's when I turn to look at the sign that's always hung up in the living room: "Benny's: Because it's all about collateral."

It smells like Old Trailer in here. Benny's not fast anymore and there is something wrong with his eyes. It's like he has to look at something twice now to see it. He is holding his side and wincing. He still has his fat wallet in his front pocket so you can't rip him off, but he's grey now, all of him. Crow had me rip a bedsheet apart into strips and is putting boiled yarrow and bear grease onto white gauze.

This will suck the poison out.

Benny got stabbed his last day in. What they laced his blade with is travelling inside of him, like porcupine quills hunting for his heart. Crow used the same medicine on my dad when his time was coming. The tattoos on Benny's hands look dusty. He has scars all over his old, shaved head.

"How much, boss?" Torchy asked.

"Eight," Benny says softly.

I draw two circles of fire touching behind my eyes so I don't forget this and realize both brothers have grown their hair long. Torchy has a scratch and poke tattoo that says "Dogrib" along one wrist to his elbow and "Forever" on the other. Both are beautiful and I bet Sfen did them.

"C or K?" Sfen asked.

Benny motioned with his lips for Crow to take the boiling pot off the burner. "K."

Crow puts a lid on the pot and we take turns marvelling at her face tattoos. She has chin stripes and the back of her hands are blurred and marked as those of a death comforter. She's marked the old way—with sinew sewn through her skin laced with suet the colour of blue—and they say her name was earned through fire.

"We work alone, Benny," Torchy said.

Benny looked at him and whispered, "Not anymore. Come back when you're done," he says.

He motions to Crow and she starts to set the table.

"Why does *Radar* have to come with us?" Torchy asks, watching me. He's called me that for years.

"My boy's here to make sure you two don't fuck up." He curls his lips. "So don't fuck this up."

The brothers listen and look at each other as they pull on their jackets. Crow puts water on for Benny's tea.

Ever since I was a kid, Benny's looked out for me. He's been gone for four years. Mom's been sick for one.

"Start my truck." He points with his lips to where his keys hang. "Flinch…"

Sfen takes them and they leave but not before I see that famous buffalo jaw hilt in the small of his back. Under his belt. Sfen: the one who loves men.

Benny runs his hand over my hand. "Jesus, look at the size of you. You got bigger. Why didn't you stay at my house?"

I'm getting fat again. This always happens before I grow even taller. I'm like a Christmas tree, Benny told me once. I zig. Then I zag. I lean down. "There was police tape."

He nods. "I'm sorry. Your heat rash is back."

He pushes my jacket back and it's true: my skin is ruddy all over me.

Crow looks up at me and I turn away. *Do not meet her gaze.*

I have this flash of Crow watching me from the trees. Not below and under. But hanging upside down from the top. Her feet broken, snapped around the branches. Her eyes open in darkness.

He nods again. "You sleep here tonight, okay? Your old room. Crow will fix something for you."

"*Mahsi.*" That would be nice. I'm at Mom's. Alone. "Why are you sending those two?" I ask.

"If Lester starts anything, let them finish it." He wheezes. "Remember what happened last time."

I make myself not. Creator, you know I'm trying to live my life like a prayer. I nod. "Sfen has a knife."

"It's for show." He squeezes my arm. "I thought about you every day."

I'm shy to look at him. We have to learn each other all over again.

"You stay with me now. Be my hands and eyes."

I nod.

"Crow," he motions. She hands me a stick of rat root. I take it, careful to not touch her hands. "Don't trust Lester. No matter what. I met a man on the inside who said Lester's got a young woman with him. A lot of your Aboriginal sisters go missing every year in Canada. They say there's a network. My buddy on the inside said men are using black medicine to snare them. Over two thousand now."

Crow stills at these words.

His eyes search her, then me. "Get that money. Speak to the girl. Check her out. Let me know what you think."

I nod and put the rat root in my jacket pocket. It's still warm from the old woman.

"You are the gentle way for me now," he says. "Crow saved my life once. She'll do it again. She's looking for an apprentice." Crow pauses as she puts the bowls out, looks down, and sighs. I don't think they're talking about me.

"I'll get your money," I say. I'm not sure what to say about the girl.

He nods and holds his side.

"Flinch," he says. "Lester has some gloves that belonged to Snowbird. Remember what he said?"

Crow stops to listen. I nod. The old man said I have ten thousand angels soaring above me, and above each one ten thousand more. All waiting, but for what?

"Bring them to us." He holds his hand to his side and closes his eyes for a long time, as if he's swallowing pain from deep within his body. "Don't let those two see or touch them, okay?"

I look to Benny. "Okay."

He points to my shovel. This is my in. "When you come back, we'll eat. I want to hear what you've been up to," he says and holds my reaching hand, giving it a careful squeeze. His grip is so weak I can almost hear the wind passing through what's left of him. He holds his side, winces. "I'm serious: I'm home now. And I'm never going back."

"Good," I say.

He winces and nods. "My boy… I'm sorry I left you."

I look to Crow and she turns from me. To this day, I can't remember if she's ever said a single word to me.

Her dogs are waiting outside. Four of them. They're huge. Built to hunt bears. I walk out and they, ears back and low, let out a growl to keep walking. Maybe those gloves could help Mom. Torchy and Sfen smoke, waiting for me. I flick my hand for them to start the truck. They do. I'm too big to sit in the cab so I hop in the back of the truck.

We ride. People are run-walking with their gloves over their faces. I don't feel it. Creator, I have never questioned why you gave me my size and the ability to not feel cold. Maybe it was so I could walk through fire for you. I asked Benny what it's like at forty below without a scarf. "It's like a dog bite to the face," he said.

Fort Simmer. Benny once said that in this town you never have to use your blinkers because everyone knows where you're going anyway. He also said the only people who ever knock here are the cops or Social Services, and that is true.

Torchy and Sfen. They used to have this battle plan when they were kids. When things were tough in their home—when their mom was being used as a human punching bag—they'd run into an old car they had in their back yard and they'd lock the doors. Sfen had a stash of Cheezies, a six pack of Coke and a blanket. That was in case they had to camp overnight.

We were friends for a summer but they were too crazy, so I let them go. I'm actually surprised sometimes that they're still alive.

I think of my mom. "Have you given her permission?" the nurse asked me yesterday. "No," I said. But then I thought about it. Yes. *She just wants to be with my dad now.*

Snowbird was a holy man. A chanter. Benny told me the day Snowbird was born seven wolves ran around his family's camp. His father, out of fear, shot the lead wolf. Snowbird was born a mute. When he was four he decided to speak to his dad. He told him, "Dad, if you wouldn't have shot that wolf, that leader. If they would have been able to come to me and speak to me and touch me, I would be able to bring the people back from the dead."

Snowbird's gloves had to be holy. The doctors had given up on helping my mom. I could tell. Last month it was *quality of care*. Now it's just *comfort*. I still wasn't sure what to do about the girl. Lester was a kind customer—a junior elder—when it came to me shovelling or hauling wood for him. He always gave me tips, sometimes gave me tea to-go with cups from the gas station. He had a stash.

Crow was different now. Their family has bone medicine. When Benny was younger, he brought her many offerings, more than anyone. My dad said it was the most curious thing: Benny brought Crow hornets' nests that had been abandoned, and Crow would nod and put them in her tent. Powerful medicine, my dad said, if you know what to do. And she did.

Benny, I guess, wanted so badly to win the snowshoe contest that my dad had always won for as long as anyone could remember. The prize was one thousand dollars and most men in town trained for months for the glory of this win. With Crow's help, Benny won. My mother asked on behalf of my father before he passed how they did it. She learned from Crow that she'd fed Benny caribou lungs and water from snow every day for four months. Maybe that was when their alliance began, for now her hair was laced with a spidery grey. When Crow came to walk her hands over the limbs of my dad and see how much time he had left, she told him a story. I was sad enough to listen but too young to remember all of it the way I learned to remember things with pictures now. She told him a story of when the world was new and how it used to be the caribou who had tusks and it was the walrus who had antlers. There was a trade and they welcomed each other into themselves.

I have always wondered since how the story went. *Why and how did they trade, Creator? And were you there as a fox?*

That was the summer Crow told my parents that I was born backwards. I felt myself fly out of my body when she said that because it was true, and I have been a ghost to myself ever since.

Maybe Snowbird's gloves will bring Benny and my mom back.

Sfen kills the lights before we turn into Lester's driveway and we stop halfway down. He's now blocked where Lester's truck should be, but it's gone. We can see the TV flickering off the walls. Someone's home. Torchy and Sfen open their doors slowly and quietly.

They motion for me to lead.

"Walk in front of me," I grab Benny's shovel and they do. Torchy gives his brother a look.

"What is a C?" I ask.

Sfen looks up to me. "What?"

"I don't know what C or K means."

Torchy lights a smoke and scoffs. He's pretending not to be afraid of me. I am twenty-two and still growing. "A C is 100. A K is a thousand."

Two circles of fire touching. Those gloves. We could save Benny. *Does Mom still want to be here?*

Do not start anything. Creator, please give me the signs to not start anything. I know they call me The Finisher, but I am here to help. I am here to free the girl.

I unscrew the light bulb outside Lester's house and Torchy nods to me to call for him. That's when I see he has a baseball bat.

"No weapons," I told him. "Don't think I didn't see your knife." I say to Sfen. His mouth opens in surprise and I can tell he doesn't want to be here.

"Never you mind, Radar," Torchy grinned. "You got your reasons for being here, and I got mine. We're getting that nine so do what you're told."

"Nine?" I said. "It's eight."

"Hell no," Sfen said. "Benny said nine."

The circles of fire touch even closer until they lock and I know they're lying, trying to confuse me. They look at each other and I feel something pass between them. It raises my skin. *Darkness.* A whispered plan.

The porch lights turn on and the brothers step back into the darkness, vanish.

"Hello?" a voice calls. "Flinch?"

I look and there Lester is, peeking out his door.

"Hi," I said. "Can I come in?"

"Sure," he said. "Everything okay?"

I hold up my shovel and nod.

I leave the shovel outside. He lets me in and I close the door behind me.

"You're out late," he smiled. "Aren't you cold?"

I nod. "I'm okay."

I stand there and look around. There are pictures all over the wall of Lester and his late wife. She was a big woman with curly hair. In each photo, Lester beams. He has his arms around her like he is holding on for dear life.

"Thanks for shovelling last week. How much do I owe you?"

"Sorry," I said.

He looks up. "Why are you sorry?"

"I'm not here for me," I said.

"Oh?" he says.

"Benny's back," I said.

His face changes. I watch it. Lester goes from being a kind old man to someone younger, someone cunning. "He's back?"

I nod.

"And you've come to collect."

I stand to my full height. *Why does it feel like there's someone else in this house—standing near me?*

"So you are the gentle way," he says.

I nod again.

"How much did he say I owe?"

"Eight grand."

He thinks about this. "I heard he got stabbed on his last day in."

I wait.

"He's hired the witch from across the river?"

I watch him as he makes his way to his freezer. I watch his hands. I watch his eyes.

"They used to be partners in fornication," he says. "Are you sure you want to be a servant with that crowd? You could work for me."

I'm quiet about this.

"How's your mom?"

I won't take the bait.

"I'm sorry," he says and he watches me. "So what happens if I don't pay up?"

"The brothers, Torchy and Sfen, are outside. Torchy has a bat. Sfen... a knife."

Lester gets a flush under his throat that warms his cheeks. "You're telling me those boys are outside?"

"They are," I say. "And Torchy wants nine grand."

"Just like that, huh?" he asks. "Benny's back and it's just like that?"

I nod. He knew this was coming. *Where is the girl?* I need to see her eyes.

"Okay," he says and shows me his hands. "I'm going to reach into the freezer. There's eight grand. I'm going to move slow. Do not hurt me. When I give you the money, I want you to give Benny a message."

I watch his hands as I open my own. "Okay."

"Tell Benny," he says as he reaches into the freezer, "that I want to play him again and tell him that we'll play double or nothing."

He knows something, I think. Lester knows something about the world now that no one else does. I can see it in him. *Creator, what is it? What have you given him or what has he stolen from you? Let me be your hands here.*

"I'll do that," I say.

And that's when the door opens behind me.

"Hello?"

It is a woman's voice. I turn and see the face of a girl my age. She stands in a fur coat. Wolf. And red high heels. Her hair is up in a bun and she has dark skin. Her lips are painted red and her eyes jet black. She is not a pretty girl. Her nose has been broken once. She is round, heavy, sad.

Where have I seen her before?

And that's when I feel something bad. Like my skin is being cut by cold and slicing ice. Like something's scraping the insides of me and pulling my guts out with sinew snapping from crooked hooks across the room and behind me. I lean quick on the counter and Lester catches that before he looks at the girl with scolding eyes.

"I filled the truck," she says. "But there's a truck blocking the driveway. I don't know what to do."

I study her and realize that she doesn't even see me. *There's something wrong with her.* Is she blind? Deaf? She looks deaf—blind halfway through her eyes maybe. That's the only way any of this makes sense.

Lester's brow furrows. "Where did you park?"

She looks through me and immediately at the floor. "Sorry. On the road. I did not know what to do so I parked it down the road. I'm sorry."

I blush at how gentle this young woman's voice is, how shy. I look at her again and realize that she is much like a younger version of the picture of Lester's wife on the fridge. Is this their daughter?

"This is Flinch," Lester says.

"Pleased to meet you," she says and holds out her hand. She doesn't look all the way up, like everyone else. "Happy full moon. I'm Crystal."

But it isn't. I take her hand. *Is she stoned?* Her fingers are so freshly painted that I can smell the nail polish. I'm not sure if I am supposed to kiss it like on TV or shake it, so I shake it once.

"Well, Flinch," Lester says and hands me a stack of cash, shrink-wrapped. "You pass along my message to Benny about double or nothin', and you tell that old squaw of his that I said hello." He looks right at me and then gives me a dirty look. "Sorry about your mom." He moves in the way of Crystal and helps her with her coat. I am being dismissed.

I leave and walk outside, puzzled. Drugs? What is wrong with her? Is she just shy? Is this medicine?

The brothers are waiting for me and I stop. "Drive. I'll meet you there."

"Did you get it?" Torchy asks.

I nod and feel so suddenly weak. "Go."

"I told Torchy it was eight," Sfen says. "I want you to know—"

"Go," I repeat.

And they leave.

Benny will be mad that I didn't get the gloves. The moment passes. *Creator, you know I did all I could here. We'll break in another time.*

I walk to Benny's and take my time. It isn't a full moon. That's the strangest thing of all. *Was that code, Creator?* I do not know if it was medicine. All I know is it was time to leave. Could I have done more for Snowbird's gloves? I think about this halfway there, scanning the shadows and trees for the brothers and their ninja ways. No. I stop and think about this. No. There was nothing I could do. There was something in the house. Or someone else. Even before she got there. Those gloves must be in there. They must. Benny was gone for four years. That's four years of hunger. Four years to dream and plan.

Benny must have called Crow from the inside. Is this about the 8K owed or is there more? A girl missing. Indian medicine. Someone's daughter. A reward or a sale to a higher bidder? What's in it for Benny? What's his "in," Creator? Show me.

I keep walking and see tracks from the brothers walking into and away from the house.

But wait: there is a third set. Someone walked behind them, after—stepping in Torchy's footsteps. The dogs growl as I kneel. I go slow and make my way.

It looks like someone came with them or came after them, but whoever this was paused three times and looked back.

Suit shoes. *Moolah* shoes. White man shoes from a store in the south.

Who could it have been?

Crow's mukluks stand in their rubbers in the porch, but I don't see her jacket. No. It will be close to wherever she is. She has gone to bed. I hand Benny his money and he takes it, thumbs it. He already looks stronger. He hands me two one hundred dollar bills from the bills I hand him. He then points with his lips to the bowl and spoon waiting for me by the pot that smells so good.

"Eat. Tell me what you saw."

"How much?" I ask.

He looks at me and acts more tired than he really is. "How much what?"

"How much are you being paid to find her?"

He looks at me and he's the old Benny, focused, hungry. "Nothing. Did you see the gloves?"

I shake my head.

"Shit. Tell me what you saw."

I take the money and grab my spoon and bowl. I move slow and think carefully of how I'll answer. He'll ask me three times to retell, retell, retell. That's how he sees. I am his eyes again. I tell him everything before I sit down and eat, even about the scraping I felt. He listens and nods and tells me to eat when I'm done. That's when I remember the one thing.

"What is it?" Benny asks.

"She said, 'Happy Full Moon.'"

"So?"

"It isn't."

"What are you thinking?"

"Maybe that was code for 'help me.'"

"I'll tell the old woman in the morning." He looks at his room. "Listen to me," he says. "There are men in the world who are taking girls and shipping them far away, making them do things you never want to see. Lester's what they call a gatekeeper to something called the Scream Factory. We're going to stop him. We're going to save that girl and then we're going to find out who he works for."

"But how?" I ask. "How do they get them?"

"They call them 'Vampires.' They're handsome men, charming men. They ask these women out on dates and, of course, the lost ones say yes. The men show up and ask to use their bathrooms. Once they're in, they're in. They get down on all fours and sniff for hair, nail clippings, Kleenex where the girls have blown their noses. Once they have something of yours, they have you. After that, you're in a spell. Soon you're giving them your PIN numbers for your cards; you're buying them a truck. You're one of maybe twelve to twenty women they have under their spell, but it's all leading the girls to something else."

I feel a cold seep into me and I don't like it. It's like we're talking about Hell, Creator. I don't like this.

And I feel that thing again: that plan. Darkness. *Over two thousand women now in the starving mouth of hell.* It passes through me and I catch a glimpse of hooks, rusty and cutting harnesses that lock, women bending backwards until the purple meat inside them bursts.

I think of Lester. His auntie is Bodacious.

"What is it?" He watches me.

"Lester. His auntie..."

"I'm meeting with her in the morning."

"Do you need me?"

He shakes his head. "Go see your mom. Tell her I said hi. Tell her I will take care of you... Tell her that we're going to start hunting the men who are hunting the women of this country."

I hang my head and nod. Did Crow tell him about how much time Mom has left?

And that's when I see it: behind him. It wasn't there before but it is now: a samurai sword in its sheath. It looks old, not the pretend kind that you can get from the head shop van that comes every summer to sell glass pipes and flags. It looks real, ancient.

"Where did you get that?" I ask.

He turns and winces. "Card game."

"When was this?"

"You just missed it," he smiled.

So that would explain the tracks in the snow. I want to ask if I can touch it but know that I can't. Not now. Not until we're done. It will be my reward to take it out and feel it.

"Things are going to happen—and I mean this with everything I know—as I get better," he says. "After your mom and after me... when you are free of this town, I want you to go to BC. I want you to work for some friends of mine. They call themselves the Night Crawlers. They're like you: superheroes. They're cleaning up the bad guys. Work for them in my name and you make this world a better place. You get on in years... the deals we make as men... the deals we make with ourselves... the deals we make with God and the world... Jesus, listen to me... these guys are doing research on this network and it's global. I've told them about you. They need a giant like you to do what you do best."

"And that is?" I ask and sit up.

"You bring peace in your own way. I've had years to think about it. In the wind of your thoughts, when you think about it... all the scores we've done. They've made the town safer, haven't they?"

I think about it. All those bad men. All that blood. All the times I hit trying to put the meat back in. "I hope so."

"My boy," he said. "There will be a day when I'm gone, when your mom is gone. On that day you will be free. Go to them. Help this world. Haunt it in my name. We both know what you are."

I don't want to understand this now. I feel something pass through me that I don't see. I take the bowl of rabbit soup and bow my head to pray. *I will eat what I have killed to touch you, Creator.*

In the night, I hear Benny cry out but it's not in pain. It's release. And I have a flash of Crow floating upside down above Benny, her long hair unbraided, sweeping over him. Her mouth open with tusks. She has four hands. Like dragonfly wings. Two we can see. Two we can't. The ones invisible reach inside him, pulling the poisoned meat out and placing a hornet's nest inside of him.

What offerings does he bring her now?

At eleven am the next morning, we pull into Lester's parking lot. Lester's truck was in the back yard. We block any escape. I sit in the back of Benny's. It starts to snow so gently and the flakes are so thick, I can light them on fire as they twirl their way down.

I step out of Benny's truck and stand behind Torchy and Sfen. Torchy looks at Benny. "You know he belongs to Bodacious, right?"

Benny takes a deep breath and holds his side. "Yup."

I wince. No matter what was agreed, this will be hard and cold, what happens next for all of us. I feel it.

Torchy spits beside him. "This is gonna cost us."

"It always does," Benny says and looks at the silver sun. It was always his favourite, he once told me. When I miss him most, I look at it for him. When he was a child, no matter what happened to him, he always had the silver sun in winter to give him hope. "We'll pay up. I've already spoken to her."

"What does she want?"

"We're to fill her freezers three times with moose and caribou."

"Wow," Torchy said.

"We'll do it." He places his hand on Torchy's shoulder, the same way he used to with me.

And that's when I know: I am no longer his disciple. He is already distancing himself from me.

"How do you want this to go?" Sfen asked.

"Watch the front of his house in case he runs," Benny says. Sfen nods and takes off in a flash. "Crow?"

Crow kneels, squints at the sky and draws her fingers through the snow. The way she holds her wrists out, it's the way women walk towards something they're about to skin and butcher. "I know what to do."

Benny looks at me and squeezes my arm. To see Crow, Torchy and Sfen working with him fills him with strength. "Do you want answers first or do you want to free the girl?" he asks Crow.

"Free the girl." She rises and speaks to the group. "He has to tell her what he did. He has to admit it."

Crow looks at the house. "Get her out here."

Lester's porch light turns on as he opens the door and stops cold when he sees us standing and that he is blocked in. "Benny," Lester said. "I was just coming to see you."

"Shut up," Benny said. "Get your skinny ass out here and bring the girl."

Lester is about to say something when he sees Torchy and me. "Fuck you guys. I paid you back—"

"Get the girl," Crow orders and Lester backs into the house.

"I fuckin' dare you to run," Torchy said.

Lester walks out of his house in his winter jacket and Kamiks. Behind him walks Crystal. She has on her fur coat and boots. I start flexing my hands. They start burning and I feel the scraping inside again.

"You sonofabitch," Benny said. "She's like a young Pearl."
Lester bows his head. "I know."

So this is why I thought I saw her before. She isn't Lester's daughter. She looks like his dead wife, but alive and younger.

Crystal turns in our direction but looks blind. "Mom?"

Crow turns to her and is quiet. She sniffs the air once.

It is Crow who walks towards Crystal. "My girl, come to me."

Crystal turns to Lester. She turns away from the group.

"My girl," Crow says. "Come."

Crystal starts to tremble in her coat and she puts her head all the way down, as far as it can go. "No."

"Lester," Crow says. "Come to me and bring her with you."

The colour drains from Lester's face. He takes Crystal's hand and walks down the stairs towards Crow. "Who fuckin' told you?" He looks at me, scathing. "The freak?"

Crow reaches out her hand. "Send Crystal to me."

"Fuck," Lester says. "I'll leave town. I'll leave today. I promise I never meant to hurt anyone. Once I started it, I couldn't stop it. I couldn't give her back. Those gloves," he says.

"I want them," Benny says.

"I burnt them," Lester says.

"You didn't," Benny says, his mouth open with disbelief.

"It's not the only way," Crow says. "Send Crystal to me."

Lester looks at Crystal and then he looks at all of us. He looks terrified. "Go to Crow, sweetie."

Crystal turns into Lester and trembles. "I'm scared."

"It's okay, sweetie," he says. "I give you permission."

Crystal walks backwards towards Crow and stops. She starts to cry. "What's happening?"

"You come now," Crow says, pointing to Lester.

Lester does as he is told. With each step, Lester ages. He drags his boots through the snow like he is on a death march. Soon, he is within grabbing distance of Crow and Crystal.

"Tell Crystal to face you," Crow says.

Lester looks at his feet. "Shit," he says.

"Do it," Crow says. "We're setting this girl free today."

Lester takes a big breath and starts to weep. "Ever since Pearl died," he starts.

"Shut up," Torchy snaps. "Do what Crow says."

"Face her," Crow says.

Lester's eyes fill with tears. "I'm sorry."

"Do it," Crow says. "You tell her. Get her to face you and you tell her what you did. Admit it."

Lester looks at the group and then at Crystal who is staring at her feet, shaking. "Crystal," he says, "face me...please."

She turns in the snow. How she moves is unnatural. It is slow motion. She looks at Lester with glassy eyes.

"Baby girl," he says. "I'm sorry."

"Tell her," Crow commands.

Crystal stares at him blankly. The life has gone from her eyes.

"I'm sorry." He swallows hard. "I used Indian medicine to get you."

She looks up at him and blinks twice. "What?" she whispers.

Lester starts to cry. "What did you say?" Crystal asks again, this time louder.

"I used black medicine to get you," Lester says.

"You did what?" Crystal asks.

"I did a bad thing," Lester says.

"You did what!" Crystal's voice breaks as she yells.

Lester starts to breathe through his nose. He begins to shake. "I lost my wife years ago and I been—"

"YOU DID WHAT?!" Crystal screams. She looks at the entire group and I watch her eyes change. They are hers again. Lester hisses when he sees this and Crystal is upon him. She digs her fingernails into his face and begins clawing and pulling. "You did what to me? You stole me? How could you? You know I have no one. You know I'm an orphan. Did you rape me? OH GOD! How could you? HOW COULD YOU?"

As she claws his face, Lester does not resist. He yells as she tears his face apart with each clawing. Blood begins to rain in spots all over Lester's Kamiks and the snow. I look away as Crystal begins to wail. I want to plug my ears so I cannot hear the sorrow in her cries. "I'm sorry," Lester keeps saying until his blood mixes with his spit. "I'm shorry."

I feel like gagging when I realize Lester is swallowing his own blood. I close my eyes when I start to hear Lester choking and gagging.

"Jesus," Sfen says. He must have come running when he heard the screaming.

"Enough," Crow says. "It's broken."

"Take her to my house," Benny says. "Torchy, Flinch, you stay."

Crow nods to Sfen. "Let's go."

I cannot look at what is left of Lester's face, but I catch a flash of meat hanging in a strip with an eye open.

"Get in the house, Lester," Benny growls.

Torchy starts pulling on skin-tight leather gloves. Black ones. He smiles and looks at Benny. Benny nods. *When things get bloody, he once told me, they get sticky.*

How long have they been working together? I wonder. *What don't I know about them?*

Benny holds my arm for support. "Get him in his house."

Torchy does as he is told. He grabs Lester and starts pulling him into his own home. Lester starts howling.

"Think of your mom," Benny looks at me. "We need those gloves."

I look at him. His eyes are changing. *No,* I think. *You need them. Just like Lester did but for something else. Something more.*

"Those gloves could save me and your mom," Benny says. I try to steer him around the blood slush from Lester's face but he chooses to step directly on it. "Let's find them."

"And then?" I ask. I have to ask now. I have to know where I stand with him. This is part of one of his plans, something bigger than I can see right now.

Benny stops. "You and I are going to go through that entire house. In his basement we will find matchboxes in a shoebox filled with hair and nail clippings from every girl he's ever stolen."

My hands go numb. *How does he know this?*

"He's the Keeper. Listen to me. Flinch, I need you to become the two-headed bear again. Call it. And we're going to find those gloves." I am so suddenly tired. All I want to do is sleep. It always starts this way when I call it—or it calls me.

My hands get numb and then the sirens start inside of me.

What did he used to call it when he was strong? His reign of blood.

"It's okay," Sfen says. "Wash the blood in the snow. Like this."

I turn and see him crouch. Sfen washes his hands in the snow and holds them up. "See?"

Crystal stands crying. She then kneels and does the same. The snow is caked with blood. I see streams of blood running out of her own fingers. Crystal has snapped her own fingernails digging through Lester's face.

The numbing travels through my legs.

"You're safe now," Sfen says. "You're safe."

Crystal begins to wail into her blood-slushed hands.

Benny walks back to his truck and slowly opens his door. He reaches behind his seats to pull the samurai sword in its sheath out. "Torchy," Benny calls. "Whatever he's used, it's in the basement. Look for shoeboxes."

I make my way into Lester's. Torchy has already turned on the oven elements. The two big ones.

Lester is zip-clipped to a chair. "Are you sure you want this?" he whispers. "Get me out of here and I'll save you."

I must have left because I don't remember if I did this or Torchy did.

I close my eyes and think. The way Crow marvelled at the girl, I know that she's found her apprentice. But the orphan is not from here. Will her community even want her back? I look around and fill my nose with how fresh and clean the snow is before I start to make my way.

Torchy comes upstairs. "There's a safe. I can't crack it."

Benny stands behind me. "Flinch?"

I nod. The bear is inside me now. Both heads. Looking.

I need to search for the signs.

I bow my head and listen. I listen with everything. The ringing starts behind my ears and behind me and moves to the front. I am vaguely aware that my hands are shaking and so are my legs. I'm vibrating across the floor.

"What the fuck?" I hear Lester say.

"That's the thing," Benny says. "That's the whole thing. My boy is a god. I've seen him reach through walls and I've seen him reach through people. By the end of the day, Lester, he's gonna reach through you."

I open my underlids.

Benny is talking but it sounds like we are in a boat and he is underneath the water.

Show me, I pray, and a voice tells me to go downstairs slowly.

Come, a voice whispers.

The basement is empty, except for a room. In it is a computer next to a printer. Beside it is a shelf. On the walls are pictures. I only look once. Lester with girls. All of the girls Native. Everyone smiling.

Sure enough, there are shoeboxes in the wall.

I reach in and look.

There are balls of hair, soft hair, nail clippings, Kleenex where girls have blown their noses. Tampons.

I am hit with the smell of dead blood.

I close the lid. I close my eyes.

I still see a picture of a girl in a harness screaming.

I close my eyes and try not to remember this but it is already too late.

There are five other shoeboxes on the shelf.

I keep the one I looked into and walk up the stairs.

"How did you—" Lester asks. "How the fuck?"

"Shhh," Benny says as I hand the box to him.

I'm weak. I lean against the wall and peek with one eye to see Benny looking in. "That's my boy. That's my miracle."

Torchy and Lester look up at me like the full mystery that I am.

"What the fuck are you?" Lester asks.

I shake my head. The bear inside of my chest looks at him with four eyes.

I don't even know anymore.

"So you're making rape-dolls now, hey, Lester?" Benny says and stands to his full height. He hands the box to Torchy who has a look. Torchy closes his eyes and puts the box down like it is haunted.

It hits me that Benny is not sick. He is not sick at all. He is just biding his time. The way he takes his breath now, he fills his whole chest like a grizzly standing tall. *Benny's home.* Just like last time. Benny didn't used to call it his "Reign of blood." He used to call it his "Rodeo of Blood." He is home now, and there is no stopping anything anymore unless it is what he wanted. He nods to Torchy who produces four long, thin knives which he places in the glowing elements.

"So this is my sword," he says. "I've been up all night researching it. It's an emperor's sword, designed to cut through three men tied up together. It's been tested."

He draws it cleanly, been practising. "Let me tell you what's going to happen next," Benny says to Lester. "I'm going to ask you three times the same question. You'll lie. Everyone lies the first two times. And I'm going to let you."

"Everybody lies, boss," Torchy smiles.

"But it's the third time I ask that's important."

"Mmm hmm," Torchy nods. A muscle in his face jumps, he is getting so excited.

"Because if you lie to me the third time, we turn Flinch on you. My boy. My attack dog. Oh the things he can do."

"My my," Torchy purrs.

"The last time someone lied, they got—what—thirty staples in their throat, chest and forehead?"

I look away and wince at the memory of the last time I unleashed myself: I tore that man's face into a starburst.

"I'm connected," Lester says, with a low growl, like a lynx in a leg hold.

"Once upon a time you was," Torchy grins. "Your Auntie Bodacious has given us until nightfall to make you talk."

And that is when Lester knows that he is all alone in the world. All alone with us in a room with the stove elements popping, four thin knives that can bore and burn their ways into anyplace, and a samurai sword. He hangs his head and starts to sob.

"Where is the place they call The Farm?" Benny asks as he unsheathes his sword. "Who are the men working together to create Blood Mares? We know this is international and it's connected to snuff and child pornography rings. We know law enforcement is probably involved—"

Lester starts rocking his chair. "No! No! No! Don't make me tell you. Don't. They'll know. They know now."

I freeze.

"They know we're talking about them. They have eyes everywhere."

"Bullshit," Benny says.

"Look," Lester says and points with his lips to the shelf. On top of it is a scrap of fabric tacked to a piece of wood. It is the eyes of a wolf that might have been on someone's T-shirt once. "They're watching right now."

"They're watching right now?" Torchy says. He gives the eyes the finger.

Lester starts to mumble and whisper something. *Is he praying?*

"Let them watch," Benny says. "Let them see the sinnery of what we're about to do to you."

It is going to be like last time. Benny asked me to tape mattresses and pillows over the windows to block the sound. I bet he and Torchy have cartons of smokes in the truck. I catch myself wincing because if this is so, then this night is just beginning. We can last for days and days, stopping only to shower and eat and plan more pain, more punishment.

"Flinch?" Benny calls.

I start to unfold. It starts like this and it's like a dogfight when I roar and hit and rip and snap, but I stop. Benny's eyes. He's scared. This is bigger than any of our "violence cures violence" campaigns.

Lester looks at all of us. "May your worst enemies raise your sons. And may your sons know the truth about all of you."

I look at Lester and feel nothing. His heart could stop halfway through my first hammer. Maybe before I even hit.

"Okay," Benny says calmly. "I'll ask again…"

I am so suddenly tired. I'm about to let go and Become when I see the time: four pm.

This is when the shift change at the hospital happens. New staff. Supper in an hour.

Mom will be wondering where I am.

I hear a voice: "Make your life holy and useful," my mom said to me this morning. "Make good choices."

She smiles. It has been weeks since she smiled.

Oh, Momma. I'm so ashamed of what these hands have done.

"Flinch?" Benny looks at me.

I look at Lester who is now looking down. I bet that to him his whole life feels like dragmarks now. He'll break quick and tell them everything.

And because of what we have opened, maybe everything for all of us now would be dragmarks.

I don't want this. I know this now.

I don't want to know any more about a place they call The Farm where they make Blood Mares. What if my size and what I am—I know I am a man of grace meant to hunt men of stone, but what about the angels Snowbird told me about? What are they waiting for?

I want my parents to be proud of me—from either side.

I want to be with my mom.

I want to hold her hand while she dreams of my dad.

"I don't belong here," I say.

"Told ya'," Torchy says. "I told you Radar would fold."

I close Lester's door and walk past Crow.

I want my life to be holy and useful.

Momma, hold on.

Crow

The girl, Crystal—who I call "Snow Light"—travels with me until we can find her people. If she is the only and last of her family, I will take her and show her what the world is forgetting. I will raise her as my own. We walk through the willows with my dogs, breaking trail back to my cabin across the ice. It will be so good to be home. We stink of town.

I think of the giant, Flinch. The helper who will one day lead. He passed the test and, when the time is right, I will tell him what we know about him.

This fills me with light.

And, again, I know that there is something starving on the way to us all. I keep moving, and I'm listening. Two sun dogs on either side of this afternoon sun watch us with pity. The one on the right is larger. This means it will only grow colder. The willows don't make a sound as we pass. On the porch of my cabin sits an old man smoking a pipe.

Snowbird.

I realize the camp is alive with children and elders, sleigh dogs and Skidoos.

This must be a celebration, I think.

"Who is that?" Snow Light asks.

"Snowbird," I said. "A friend."

My heart sings as my dogs growl.

"Hush," I say.

I squint to look at Snowbird and a red fox sits beside him. She looks at me and him. He says something before she leaves but not before looking back once, twice, to see me.

She leaves and I feel pure.

But I still have that haunted feeling.

We are still being watched.

It's as if the face of the forest, the ears of the Creator, are listening. War is coming. All of my dreams point to this.

As we get closer, more elders come from their camps and are coming to meet us.

Each one is a healer and a carrier of bundles, medicines, ceremony.

As happy as I am that a gathering of Holy People has been called, I can still smell blood.

I look to the four directions. I can see the water tower of Fort Simmer.

War is not only coming to the north, but it is coming for the world.

May the snow forgive us all.

A ho.

If Only Tonight

As the David Gray CD wound down for the second time in a row, Lance marveled again at the most beautiful star blanket shining away over the spot where the James Wedzin painting used to hang in Duane and Juanita's living room. The pattern was violet and gold. It vibrated—*no*—*it hummed*, Lance thought, so loudly in how it presented itself that he had to look away. He felt his eyes cross every time he tried to focus on it.

He wondered if the James Wedzin painting he'd commissioned with two tents in a northern meadow had been taken by Duane when he left or if it was under the blanket.

As Shari and Juanita talked in the kitchen, Lance sipped his coffee and marvelled at how beautiful they looked tonight: spring dresses, hair down, ankle bracelets sparkling over their right ankles, nails done, glowing. *You'd never guess one of my goddesses was fighting for her life*, he thought. He glanced at the star blanket and remembered asking James Wedzin to add the second tent to the meadow so Duane and Juanita would always know he and Shari would never be far away from them as couples, as family. As MC for their wedding three years ago, Lance presented the painting with Shari at his side with the words, "You can always count on us for help. The good times and the growing pains. We will be there for you both."

And they embraced.

Now, as Lance looked around the home, it looked like Juanita had been robbed. The George Littlechild, the Susan Point, the Chris Paul—all of the big paintings that used to hang proudly in Duane and Juanita's home were gone.

Duane had left Juanita. Tonight, during supper, Lance observed half of Juanita's music and art collection gone, and it felt official. Duane had not told Lance why, nor were there any real warning signs. Juanita had returned a week ago from her photo shoot to half a home. Duane had choreographed a moving truck and helpers for when his wife was at an appointment.

You think you know someone, Lance thought as he looked at Juanita and felt an ache for her. *Duane, you fucking coward.* What a horrible year. Juanita had been diagnosed with breast cancer. He wasn't entirely clear how, but the date for a double mastectomy was looming and, just when Duane should have been there to hold and comfort his wife, he'd simply vanished.

Lance had tried Duane's cell, his e-mail, his work. Duane was gone. When he thought about it, were the signs there? He and Shari had been in their own whirlwind of realizing they were pregnant and then losing the baby ten weeks in. To cope, he'd hurled himself into teaching and his own work of gathering stories, so he'd missed the last three sweats at UBC. He hadn't seen Duane in weeks. *Weeks*, he pondered. *Was that all it took for a marriage to unhinge?*

His own distance with Duane had started well over a year ago. The gang had a ritual: to meet every second Sunday at a new diner for brunch. The deal was one person paid for everyone and they took turns reading the "Savage Love" sex advice column out loud to the others. Over the past few years, quite a few of the articles no longer applied to them.

"We're too vanilla now," Lance joked.

"It's starting to feel that way," Shari agreed.

And they laughed. Yes, fisting, golden showers and orgies didn't really apply to any of them, but these reading sessions that used to be hilarious or juicy, now, for the past few months, had added a tension to the table.

Lance should have realized that this was exposing the valley between Juanita and Duane—long before the diagnosis.

"Lance," Juanita called. "How's your coffee?"

He looked at her and smiled. "Perfect. So can I ask the obvious: where do you think Duane is?"

Shari gave him her firm look, the one that stated that this was not the time.

Juanita looked at them both. "Let me go pee and we'll talk, okay? We're celebrating four glorious things tonight—maybe more, but let me get prepared, okay?"

Shari put her hand on Juanita's shoulder. "Pee, Sister. Pee."

Juanita left and Shari whispered, "Is this the best time?"

Lance shrugged. "Don't you want to know what happened?"

"Of course I do," she said. "What a fucker."

She went back to doing the dishes.

Celebrating four glorious things? he thought. That was strange: Juanita had asked that both he and Shari bring songs that mattered deeply to them, but she also asked that they save telling each other which song it was. Lance had brought "If only tonight we could sleep" by the Cure because it brought him into complete surrender every time he listened to it. He'd trance out and remember the first time he and Shari made love: looking into each other's eyes, he asking himself if this was really going to happen. He'd been crazy about her for over a year before he asked her out, so he didn't want to wreck anything. The first time he made love to her, he didn't hold back. He took his time kissing her, going down on her, tasting her. She marvelled at him and told him so, after.

"Wow," he remembered her laughing into her pillow. "I'm so sorry I went preverbal there. Wow."

Lance, even now, nodded at the memory. "Need help?" he asked.

"No," she said, "you cooked. Rest."

She gave him her doe-eyes. "What are you thinking about over there? Where did you go just now?"

"Oh," he said. "I'm just thinking about the first time you let me make love to you."

She laughed. "Shhhh."

He winked at her and felt the blood rush at the thought of them lying together in their home, with all of the windows open to create a warm breeze. Her cool body against his, cuddling, dreaming. He marvelled at his wife. Not only was the miscarriage something they honoured together, Shari had said the day after, "Now we know we can have a child, Lance. Thank you. Bring me our daughter. I can see her out of the corner of my eye. She's waiting. I feel like this was a test run and we passed. Now we know. This is our time to build our nest before she comes."

She had touched his face at Kits Beach in a new way. He couldn't name it, but Shari was a new woman now. They would conceive and they would begin their family. This was their time to celebrate their fertility. Lance had had his vasectomy reversed and the anguish that he was not fertile was no longer a worry. He was "firing live" as his doctor said, and he and Shari were trying again.

Most wonderfully, Lance thought, was a message that came to him when they were both receiving acupuncture from a fertility specialist. Lance was drifting when the softest voice spoke to him. It said simply, "When you make love with her body, make love to her spirit." He woke from the deepest island inside himself and had not told her this. It was his secret that he would share later.

Tonight, they'd just shared a feast of fresh sockeye fried in his famous lemon and butter sauce to blackened perfection—both Shari and Juanita loved the skin to be charred—on a bed of garlic and lemon couscous, some garlic mashed potatoes and one of Shari's avacado salads. Lance was so proud of himself as he'd cooked most of it. He'd used flour and a mix he'd created himself out of herbs from the local farmers' market. Now he sipped his favourite coffee. It wasn't Starbucks or Timmies: it was the Safeway Breakfast Blend. Every sip took him back to when he and Shari first got together in his tiny apartment and the days that would blur into one another of music, reading together, sex, walks, feasts, concerts. He rarely vacuumed his hardwood floors as they were covered in sand from Kits Beach, and he thought that waking to sand in your toes was one of the sexiest things in the world. He'd brought a pound of coffee with him tonight and decided he'd leave it so every time they came back to check on Juanita it would be a comfort. She'd need a lot of help in the months ahead. Not just with Duane but with the surgery and the everything after. And they'd be there. He'd already told his department head, Brian, what was going on and arrangements were already in place to get him out of the classroom and away from a few of his other obligations. Brian had lost his own wife three years earlier to breast cancer, so he told Lance to be careful, since

Brian's wife had had all the assurances that she was going to make it, but three months later was gone.

Juanita came out of the bathroom wiping her hands on her dress. She carefully took her favourite mug—a smiling sun with two stars beside it—from the table, walked across the living room and sat across from Lance in her favourite chair. Beside it were her books. She was always reading three or four at a time and she curled her legs up beside her. She was not only tanned, she was glowing. Vancouver's summer sun had lightened a few strands of her hair and this only brought out her foxlike features and her freckles on the nose and cheeks. Lance had always had a quiet crush on Juanita, and it bloomed now as she sat across from him.

Shari sat beside him and held his hand. He put his coffee down and waited for Juanita to speak.

"Can I tell you about this star blanket?"

Lance nodded and he felt Shari's feet wiggle under his leg. He couldn't resist: he took his free hand and wrapped his fingers around the curve of her ankle.

Juanita looked at the star blanket and ran her fingers along the fabric of her seat. "When I was about 14, I used to play spin the bottle with my friends and a couple of kids from the rez at an older girl's house. It was fun. If you spun on a girl, you kissed a girl. If you spun on a boy, you kissed him. 'Seven Minutes in Heaven' was the grand finale. It all led up to that. That was four people the bottle chose that had to go into this huge closet and make out for seven minutes."

"Four people?" Shari asked. "Wow."

"Sounds like fun," Lance said.

"It was. I often think back to that time. I couldn't wait for Fridays to roll around."

"Why Fridays?" Shari asked.

"Bingo. I guess some would call us 'Bingo orphans' but we took care of each other."

Lance had a flashback of a younger Juanita kissing other girls. Finding the faces of boys in the dark. Tongues and breath. Breasts cupped through shirts and under. The first time you felt the warmth of someone's tummy. Fingers finding their way to heat and wetness. The discovery of fur and how someone tastes.

"So we had fun, but our host, Lisa, for whatever reason, never got chosen by the bottle for anything. It would literally pass her by every single time. It became a bad joke and she'd always be outside the closet for our make-out sessions, so one day we went to her home and she had a star blanket like this but bigger waiting in the back yard. We all asked, 'Hey, what's this? Are we playing outside tonight?'

"Lisa had a different plan, a new plan. She said, 'Let's try something new. Rather than all of us waiting to be chosen, why don't we throw this blanket up in the air and we all run under and we make out for a whole hour?'"

Juanita ran her fingers through her long, thick hair and smiled. "We all looked at each other and realized what she was proposing: a full-on semi-clothed orgy for one whole hour. She'd cleared all the rocks so it was the softest grass and she had the tallest fence so no one would see us. It was just us. Our circle. I think there were just as many boys as there were girls and all of a sudden we got quiet. None of us could believe what was about to happen. The next thing I knew, we all held the corners of the star blanket and threw it up in the air before hitting the ground and making out. I remember she even set her dad's alarm clock. She had two extension cords hooked up and everything. She played the Eurythmics on a ghetto blaster. Touch was the album. I get goosebumps every time I listen to it. We all had to swear we'd never tell anyone what was happening and we did that all summer. Every Friday. It was hot. Making out with two or three people at once. Being held. Touched. Groped. We had this biter. Amanda. Her bites got harder as she lost herself. It was hysteria and hunting all at once. That summer saved me. It got me through a lot. I told that story to my angel on Cancer Connections and she mailed me this blanket."

Lance reached for his glass of water and realized he'd been holding his breath at this story. It was magic. He saw that the book on top of Juanita's pile was The Breast Health Book, her Bible as she called it. He could see pressed flowers of all kinds used as bookmarks.

"Wow," Shari said. "You did that all summer?"

"We did," Juanita said and sipped her tea.

"I would have loved that," Shari said and touched Lance's face. "I know someone else here who would have loved it, too." She wiggled her toes under his leg.

Lance blushed and looked down. He could feel a new spirit in the room: one that welcomed questions. "So where did Duane go?"

Juanita took a big breath and looked down. "Oh, he's fucking one of his Iowaska sisters."

"What?" Lance and Shari asked together.

Juanita nodded. "I should have known. We had sex once every two days for years and it just tapered off. His phone went off in the middle of the night a few weeks ago, and it was like he was on fire to get out of the room and turn it off."

"How long has this been happening?" Lance asked.

"Long enough, I guess," Juanita sighed. "I guess old Enaud didn't want a breastless woman around so he traded me in for a new and younger model."

"Enaud?" Lance asked.

"I read one of the e-mails his Iowaska sister wrote. Apparently, Duane had a vision in one of their ceremonies where he saw his name backwards and now he only answers to Enaud in their little group."

Lance felt his cheeks burn. "How sad."

"I'm so sorry," Shari said.

"It's not your fault," Juanita said. "You've had a tough spring."

Lance looked to Shari and it was true. Juanita had been there through it all. Where had Duane been? Well, Lance thought. Wasn't it obvious?

Shit! Lance felt suddenly furious with Duane. Why the hell didn't he tell him he and Juanita were in trouble? The last time they'd been together was at the Commodore Ballroom to see a show, but, even then, there hadn't been a lot of conversation. Just the standard, "Here we go" when the band took the stage and, after, a brief hug goodbye as they were parked in different spots downtown. They walked away quickly as they both had to work early the next morning.

Lance let out a sigh. When he thought about it, the last few times he and Duane had gone for coffee, Duane had spent a lot of time checking his e-mails and texting, and there was a distance between them. When Lance thought about it, Duane had never been fully present after the miscarriage. He'd stopped by with Juanita and visited for a bit, but when was the last time they'd had a heart-to-heart—months?

"The good news," Juanita said, "is my portraits are in."

"They are?" Shari asked. "Can I see?"

"Portraits?" Lance asked. "Oh—portraits!" He remembered.

"I'd love to see them," Shari said.

Juanita winked at them both. "I've hung the portraits up in our... my room."

The day Juanita returned to find Duane gone, she'd gone off to a photographer on Oak and 16th who did the most gorgeous portraits of women and their breasts. Juanita wanted photos of herself topless and beautiful. Lance wasn't sure if he was allowed to ask to see them. He deeply wanted to. He adored Juanita as a friend and woman, but he was also so scared for her.

What if she was gone in a few months?

Juanita and Shari were both slender with powerful bodies. Summer had darkened both of them, though Shari had more freckles. For cup size, they were pretty well matched, Lance thought and Shari's breasts were beautiful: not too big, not too small. Shari's Chipewyan nipples would be darker, but...

Lance sat up as he felt himself getting aroused knowing that he may get a privileged revenge-viewing now that all bets were off with old Enaud.

"I'd love to see these," Shari said. "I'm sure Lance would, too." She gave Lance a wink.

Lance blushed and looked down.

"Well," Juanita smiled. "Perhaps you'll both get to, but I have a question first."

"It's your night," Shari said. "Ask away."

"Lance," Juanita said. "You told us a story once. I want you to tell it to me again."

"Story?" Lance frowned. "Which one?"

"The one about you in college. Your roommate."

"You know," his wife said. "The sleepwalker."

"Oh," Lance blushed. "The sleepwalker."

"Yes," Juanita said. "I don't think you ever told us the whole story. I want to hear it again."

Shari levelled her eyes at him. "Yes, that is one of the most curious stories you've ever told. I would like to hear it, too."

Lance reached for his water. "I don't want to get into trouble."

"Oh come on," Shari said. "This was way before you knew me. You have diplomatic immunity."

"We're under the Star Blanket of Trust," Juanita added. "Consider this a dare from a dear friend. And it's a full moon out. I want you to tell the story, the whole story and don't leave anything out."

Lance felt himself gulp for air. This was a dangerous story because it was scandalous with its perceived innocence. He looked at his wife. "Okay, but if I tell it, nobody can get mad at me. This was when I was, like, 21. I was totally single and innocent."

"Oh yes," Shari nudged him playfully. "Mister Innocent. Plus, it's a dare."

Juanita giggled and Lance knew he had to tell the story.

He took a big breath and ran his palms back and forth over his legs to get going. "Okay, so there was this one summer where I was in college. All of the guy roommates went home for the summer, and I decided to stay and work for minimum wage and enjoy the city. But we had this one foreign student who moved in to help pay rent."

"Did she have nice feet?" Shari teased.

"Baby," Lance said and looked down.

"Oh come on, Lance," Juanita said. "Everyone knows you love feet."

Lance blushed again, this time deeper in his cheeks, hotter.

"Baby," Shari said softly and pushed her left foot into his hand. He held it and felt himself getting so turned on. He nodded.

"She was beautiful, but I was totally not in her league in any way. I couldn't even speak to her."

"You? The charmer?"   •

He shook his head. He loved how the two women he loved dearly were waiting to hear this story—all of it—this confession of confessions. Would he tell it all? It was a dare and he did have diplomatic immunity. He took a big breath. "I think it was the second night. Vancouver was in a heat wave. The second night she'd moved in she came into my room and started wrestling me with her bra and panties on. It wasn't a fight. It was this struggle. I slept naked so I had no idea what was going on. She started riding me and struggling but her eyes were closed. God, she was strong. She'd hold me down and ride me through her panties, and I'd have to keep her from grabbing and pulling my hair. It was crazy."

Both Juanita and Shari started laughing.

"Then, just as quickly as it started, it stopped. She just stood up and left. She literally just stood up when I got hard and she went into her room. The next morning she acted as though nothing happened. It happened on the third night. I think at around two in the morning. She'd go out dancing with her friends and come home to me and this whole riding ritual would start."

"Wait," Shari said. "Were you inside her through her panties?"

Lance frowned. "Maybe. All I know is it gave me a backwards boner."

The ladies burst out laughing. Lance shook his head and kept going. "It just seemed as soon as I got hard she'd leave. The whole point was to wrestle me and rub against me just enough and then she'd leave."

"Wow," Juanita said.

"I'm starting to hear some new information here," Shari said. "Keep going."

"Uh oh," Lance said. "Am I in trouble?"

"Baby," Shari said. "It's a full moon. You didn't even know me then. Full diplomatic immunity, remember?"

He and Shari laughed as this was an old joke between them.

"Hurry," Juanita said. "Get to the juicy."

Lance ran his fingers through his hair and took a quick sip of water. "Okay. Okay. I think it was around day four of this when I finally said, 'Can we talk about what happens at night?' To which she acted totally shocked. 'Oh no,' she said. 'Am I sleepwalking?' 'Sleep Wrestling more like it!' I said, and she started to cry. 'Oh no,' she said. 'When I drink or when I get stressed, I sleepwalk or sleep wrestle.' It happens during exam time. One time I woke up in a tent I'd assembled in the next door neighbour's yard. Apparently, I can read directions in my sleep. The only problem is it doesn't matter if I'm clothed or not. Was I naked?'"

"'No,' I said. 'You're in your bra and panties.' 'I'm so sorry,' she said. 'I can move out. I'll find a new place.' 'No,' I said. 'You don't have to. It's just that you pull my hair and press down on me so hard I get headaches after.' 'Oh God,' she said. 'I'm so ashamed.' And she hugged me. 'My parents are so worried I'll walk out into the city naked and end up Lord knows where.'"

"Holy shit I love this story," Juanita cheered. "So, dear Lance, whatever did you do?"

Lance smiled. "Well, I couldn't turn her out into the cold cruel world, could I?"

"No you could not," Shari beamed. "Dear husband, please carry on."

"Well," Lance smiled. "I was there for her during that summer. She was under a lot of stress and came into my room each night to wrestle me. Could I help it if I slept naked? Could I help it if sometimes she was naked? I had to protect her."

Lance felt his erection build. He wiggled and was aware both women caught that. He cleared his throat. "It was a great summer for both of us."

"But how did you know it was consensual?" Shari asked.

"Well," Lance said. And the truth was he honestly could not remember what he'd shared before, so he decided to go for it and share it all. "At first, she'd press into me and get me hard and leave. But, after her confession, she'd come in without any undies on, already wet. It was like the air could taste her."

He stopped. *Where did that line come from?*

"Wow," Juanita said. "Go on."

"Well, I'd always be under her and she had this hair pulling thing she did that I hated but, soon, she'd rub against me and cum from brushing. It was riding without penetration and she'd lay off the hair pulling if I sucked on her tits or licked her nipples, but she'd stop as soon as she came and she'd leave."

"Did you ever get to cum?" Juanita asked, genuinely concerned.

"No," Lance said and felt his voice lighten with arousal. "I never did."

"Oh, poor Lancey," Shari said and squeezed his thigh. "Talk about a cruel summer."

He shrugged and remembered her body. She had pink nipples. Tiny ones that swelled to twice their size. He loved to push her breasts together when she was on top and lick them back and forth as if they were one. "I learned to take care of myself, shall we say." Both women giggled. "And I lived for the night. Man, she was strong." He didn't need to close his eyes to remember what a gorgeous body she had. Alicia was her name. From Italy? Yes, he was sure it was Italy. Or maybe Sicily. Wait. Maybe it was Madrid. She'd trimmed her muff so she could wear sundresses but her lips were bare. He remembered the very tip of her was soaked with her own juices and there was a night where she actually climbed on his face and ground herself into his nose and mouth until she climaxed before climbing off and going to bed. He remembered walking like a blind man to the bathroom to wash her off of his face and being shocked there was so much of her. He loved it.

"So you two never did it?" Juanita asked.

"No," Lance shrugged. "I don't think it was about that. I don't think either of us were ready for sex. This was a way around it."

"So how did you two leave each other?"

Lance thought about it. "She got into another program and her time was up. I drove her to the airport and she gave me a long hug. When I returned home, she'd left me a gift. A pair of her see-through panties under my pillow. The ones she used on several night visits. The ones she came in fastest."

"Wow!" Juanita said and started clapping.

"So what did you do with the panties?" Shari asked, and her voice was the inquisitive voice, the one that wanted the absolute truth, the one that would know the exact second he fibbed.

Lance decided to push it. "I... shall we say...I relaxed in a gentlemanly way... for months with them."

"Around your cock?" Juanita asked.

Both Shari and Lance looked at Juanita and started laughing out of shock.

"Juanita," Shari said. "You've never said that word before."

"Well, that story gets me so horny just thinking about it. How could I not?"

Shari looked at Lance with surprise. *Wow*, she mouthed.

Lance felt bewildered. "Um, so the question is?"

"My question is, Lance, did you beat off with it around your cock or did you beat off sniffing it?"

"Both," Lance said and felt something leave his body.

Shari looked at both of them. "Whoah."

They were all quiet.

"Wow," Shari said again, to the story or to this new spirit in the room: Juanita's arousal and power.

"You know," Juanita said, sipping her tea. "You two saved our sex life."

"What?" Shari asked. "How?"

Juanita sat up. "If this is my night, I want to tell you both. I've always had problems cumming. I take forever sometimes."

Shari and Lance nodded.

"But when old Enaud and I would have sex, I had this image of you two—all these years—this one image that would push me over. That's what I'd call it. I'd build and build and you two would help me."

"What was it?" Shari asked and reached for Lance's hand. He took it and squeezed gently.

"Well," Juanita said. "If this is my night and I have diplomatic immunity I'll tell you, but I need wine first."

"Is this wise?" Shari asked.

"Sister," Juanita said. "They're going to take my breasts. If there was ever a night for wine and enchantment, this is it—plus it's a full moon. Do we not all have diplomatic immunity tonight under our auntie in the sky?"

Shari cleared her throat. "I'd love a glass with you."

Lance looked at Juanita in a new way: she was free now. On her own. Everything she'd wanted to do, she now could. She truly had nothing to lose.

He felt Juanita's eyes on him and he looked away. This had been happening over the past year: an awareness of one another. There had been an afternoon in the Farmers' Market on Granville Island where he and Shari had joined Duane and Juanita for some Christmas shopping. In the grand push and pull of the crowd, Lance had reached out to run the back of his hand along the inside of Shari's wrist and hand—only to realize he'd done this to Juanita and she'd not resisted or stopped him. In fact, they'd easily had seconds holding hands like lovers together before he jumped out of shock and apologized to Juanita, but she'd only smiled and turned away to continue shopping. He'd wanted to tell Shari about it but felt that it was an innocent mistake, but, still, it was a sharing. Juanita's skin was so soft. He realized that the only time they ever touched was in their welcome and until-next-time hugs. What happened on Granville Island was skin on skin, and it had been an uncurling of a hand into the soft wrist of a woman he adored. And she let him.

"Honey, are you okay over there?" Shari asked as she poured the wine into a long stemmed glass.

Lance nodded. "Perfect." His voice cracked and they all laughed.

Lance could feel the hottest blood inside himself floating near the top of his skin. He took a deep breath and realized that his body was filled with the hottest and most exquisite humming. His chest felt tender underneath his shirt and he found himself breathing through his mouth. His body was purring with arousal and what would happen next.

"You know, Lance," Juanita said. "Women talk."

Lance smiled and spoke softly. "No...really?"

Juanita giggled.

"Wait," Shari said and returned with the wine. She handed one to Juanita and kissed the top of her head softly. "For you."

"Thank you," Juanita said and they touched glasses so quietly.

Shari sat down and kissed Lance before turning to Juanita. "What was this about us saving your sex life?"

Both women raised their glasses and sipped slowly.

"Yum," Juanita said. "Oh yes. Duane or Enaud always complained I was never wet enough. We always had to use lube. I could see it when we'd have to stop halfway through to find the bottle. I made the mistake of reminding him once of something called foreplay and he never let me forget it. With him, it was always same thing: missionary or doggy style with minimal anything before or after."

Lance imagined that and found himself rolling deeper into arousal. This was getting closer to something growing between all of them.

"I thought you said he was a cuddler," Shari said.

"Oh he was," Juanita said. "Old Enaud was a great cuddler. He's probably cuddling someone named Lisa right now."

"Oh fuck Lisa. Let's keep this going," Shari said. "I'm really interested in what image you have of Lance and me that helped 'push you over.'"

"Well," Juanita said and took a sip of her wine. "Old Enaud liked to watch a little porn to get in the mood. At first, I tolerated it but, after a while, I liked to watch, too. There's this one woman—I can never remember her name. I have a crush on her. I love watching her. The image I have of you both is that while Duane was fucking me, Lance…" Juanita stopped and covered her face. "Oh I can't say it. I'm too shy."

Lance let his breath out at the same time Shari did.

"It's okay," Shari said. "Full diplomatic immunity, remember?"

"Whew!" Juanita said and looked up to the ceiling. "Okay, but you can't look at me when I tell you. I'll get too embarrassed."

"Okay okay," Shari laughed. "Lance, let's look away."

Lance felt his face burn with excitement. He looked at the star blanket.

"Are you looking away?"

"We are," Shari called. "Where are you looking?"

"Into a pillow," Juanita said. "The bunny one I gave you—from the Smoking Lily."

"The one I picked out," Lance said with a shiver. His cocked ached with hot blood-arterial blood—finding its way in a waterfall of arousal as it began coursing through his entire body.

"So as Enaud would be fucking me, I'd imagine …Oh my God! I can't say it!" And she started to laugh. Then Shari started. Then Lance started. It was a laugh from the heart. They laughed and laughed and until they were all out of breath and Lance felt his wife curl her toes under his leg.

"So blah de blah and blah de blah," Juanita raised a glass. "And I would come every single time."

Lance let out the biggest breath and pressed his palms into his eyes. "Okay. Wait. You cannot cheap out on us like that."

"Oh yes I can," Juanita said. "I just did!"

"Juanita..." Shari said, "you're turning me on. Don't hold back now."

"I can't!" Juanita yelled with a smile. "I can't say it. We just have to do it, okay? No words. There are no words for how I can explain it. We just need to do it. Together. As friends."

"Oh God," Lance thought and rubbed his hands together quickly, as if starting a fire the old way. *"This is it. This is what's been building all night."*

Lance knew Shari had fooled around with women when she was younger. She'd had a girlfriend one summer who kept in touch years later on Facebook and Lance did not mind at all. To think of his tough Dene wife making love to another woman was something special to him, something they never needed to talk about.

"You know," Juanita said. "I've always felt that when men marry, they find invisible wives along the way. Sometimes it's at work, sometimes it's through friends, but, Lance, I've always considered myself to be your invisible wife."

Lance looked down. He felt her words blanket him but didn't know what to say. He was suddenly terrified he'd lose her. *Too soon,* he thought. *What she was now facing had come too soon. But she would not fight it alone. He and Shari would do whatever it took to help her.*

"I've told Shari this and I don't know if she told you," Juanita said.

Lance felt a tear slide down his face. "She hasn't." Why was he crying? He was, out of surprise and dread. He wiped his eyes. Shari squeezed Lance's hand that this was okay. This was important. Everyone knew there was a chance Juanita would not survive her operation. She'd lost her mother to breast cancer and an auntie had passed away on the operating table. Her heart had simply stopped. Perhaps out of heartbreak at the thought of losing her breasts.

Lance dry swallowed and nodded. "Thank you."

"No, thank you. You've always been there. Both of you."

"You know," Shari said. "I believe all these years, Juanita, you've been my invisible wife, too."

Juanita smiled. "Really?"

"You carried me through the infertility years and our miscarriage. I've always loved you. You taught me to dress, to do my hair. You were my sister but also my wife. I've had my thoughts over the years. You have a beautiful body, an exquisite body. I've had my thoughts of you when Lance and I were making love."

"You have?" Lance and Juanita asked together.

"Oh yes," Shari said. "Lance, do I have diplomatic immunity?"

"Of course," Lance said.

"Ummm… okay," Shari said. "I sometimes pretend that when we fuck, Lance is you but with a cock."

Lance heard himself inhale at the boldness of this, the perfection of this.

"Wow," everyone said together and it was like the room exhaled together. Lance felt the hottest deepest blood inside himself swell through him once again.

"I like that," Juanita said. "I like that a lot."

The women—his goddesses—raised a glass and drained the rest of their wine.

"And, Lance," she said. "I've always loved your eyes. They're so tender, so sincere. But they're fierce, too. It turns me on the way you look at Shari. I can tell that you are her wolf."

Lance blushed. "Thank you."

"Don't you just want to grab his sideburns and fuck his face?" Shari asked.

Juanita burst out laughing. "I've thought about it."

Lance blushed and looked down. He was speechless.

"Mmm," Shari purred. "This feels nice." She laughed and ran her fingers through her husband's hair. Lance felt both honoured and deliciously shocked.

"Can we see your pictures?" Shari asked. "Your portraits?"

Juanita thought about it. "Maybe. They're upstairs in my bedroom."

My bedroom, Lance thought. It's all hers now.

"Before I show you," Juanita said, "I wanted to let you in on a secret."

"Oh?" Lance and Shari looked at each other.

"The four things we're celebrating?" Lance asked.

"Yes. I've been working on something," Juanita said.

"In secret?" Shari said.

"Yup," Juanita said, "and I wanted to share some incredible news with you—but you can't tell anyone."

"What is it?" Lance asked.

"Well," Juanita said slyly. "I've been working on a dream of mine ever since my diagnosis and it looks like it may have taken off in a good way."

"What is it?" Lance and Shari asked.

"I'm glad you asked," Juanita said. She pulled out a T-shirt that read, "Unless it makes my nipples sing or helps find the cure for all cancers, I don't want to hear about it."

Shari and Lance laughed.

"Cool shirt," Lance said. "Where did you get it?"

"I made it," Juanita beamed. "It's being picked up by an organization and it'll be used to help fundraise."

"Congratulations," Shari said.

Juanita threw one to both of them. "You get the first ones. We launch this next week."

"Good for you," Lance said. "When did you do this?"

"The same time I worked on this," She said as she reached behind her chair and she pulled out a large green bowl. Lance had seen this one before. It was a wedding present, made out of bamboo. It was usually holding gluten-free chips or nachos.

She passed the bowl to Shari and motioned with her chin. "Take one and pass it to Lancey."

She smiled and winked at both of them.

Shari took the bowl, reached in and swirled her hand around. She plucked a note and was about to read it when Shari said, "Not yet. Now Lance gets to pick one."

Lance was handed the bowl and he could see that each note was typed up professionally and on the back in silky, purple letters were the words: DARE: *What's a little desire between friends?*

"Turn it over and read it," Juanita said. "Shari first."

Shari turned her card over and, by candle light, Lance saw his wife's eyes widen. She laughed and covered her mouth.

"What?" Lance asked. "What is it?"

"Oh I can't," she said. "I can't—I can't!"

Lance looked at his wife. Then he looked at Juanita. "What is it?"

"So," Juanita said. "What I'm hearing from you, my dear, is that you're not going to answer the question or complete the dare?"

Shari shook her head. "I will not. Not now—not ever."

She tucked the card back into the bowl and mixed it up. She covered her face with both hands and started laughing. "What is this game?"

"It's called DARE," Juanita said. "I invented it."

"What!" Lance and Shari said together.

"Yup," Juanita beamed, "and a board game company has decided to launch it. This is our prototype.'"

Lance and Shari's jaws dropped.

"What?"

"That's incredible!" Lance said.

"You're amazing!" Shari echoed.

They both started clapping. They rose and hugged Juanita and she hugged them back gently. Lance noticed that she was protecting her chest. He closed his eyes and held her a little longer than usual. *Dear Lord*, he thought. *Don't let us lose you. Please, God.*

He swallowed hard and looked down.

"Oh now," Juanita said. "Your turn, Lance."

Lance turned his card around and read aloud the words as he discovered them, "What is the one thing your lover has told you about yourself that turns them on that you had no idea before you met them?"

Lance sat down and sipped his water. He looked to his wife and repeated the question.

Shari beamed. "Answer please."

"Well now," Lance said. "I would have to say that I had no idea that my hands were sexy."

Both women started laughing.

"I could have told you that," Juanita said and she winked at Shari.

Lance realized that this was not news to either of them. He reached out and kissed Shari. "Thank you, sweetie."

"No, baby. Thank you! They are sexy hands—especially when you're holding me after we make love."

"Or when you're cooking for us," Juanita said and sipped her wine. She gave him a special smile.

Lance felt something excruciatingly exciting building in the room. It felt freeing and alive.

"What is this game?" Lance asked.

"Well," Juanita said. "The gift of cancer is that you put things into perspective right away. You realize that all we have is right now. I decided that I wanted to create a board game or a card game that dared couples to risk their vulnerability. Sooner or later, we all forget about spinning the bottle as adults—and even when we're in love. So I invented Dare and I've thought up about 200 questions."

"Baby," Lance looked to Shari. "What card did you get?"

"Darling," she said coolly to him, "I may tell you later if you're a good boy." She then looked at Juanita. "You know what card I picked, don't you?"

Juanita shrugged. "I think I do."

"So you're telling me that you'd do it?"

"Of course I would—if I was dared."

"Where did you even think of that?"

Juanita blushed. "I have certain guy friends and there are certain forums where there are people who are into that."

Forums? Lance thought. *Yum yum. What has Juanita been up to at nights?* he wondered.

"So you'd do it?" Shari asked. "You'd do it right now?"

"Yes!" Juanita yelled. "I would. I mean I'd love for five minutes to prepare myself and I'd love to choose the lighting, but I would."

"What was the dare?" Lance asked as he reached into the basket and took a few cards. He turned them over.

1. When was the last time you came? What did it feel like? Describe it to us.

2. Thirty second dare: get your friends to do whatever you want them to for only 30 seconds. Quick. Don't think. Dare them.

3. Use the silk handkerchief to gently secure someone so they can't see and play "Where will I kiss you next?" You have as many kisses as you wish. Make one tickle; make one ache and make one count. Go!

4. What do you think "second base" is for a girl? Don't hold back and act it out. GO!

Lance felt his breath catch with all of this. He also felt himself blush. His chest tightened in full arousal and he put the cards down. *My God*, he thought. *What a treasure.*

"Oh you just hold on," Shari said and started to laugh. "So," she levelled her eyes at Juanita. "You'd do it right now if I dared you."

Juanita nodded. "I would."

"Jesus," Shari sat down and tucked her feet under Lance's legs. "This woman is fearless."

Everyone laughed. Lance agreed. He was tempted to keep reading the 80 or so cards all marked DARE but decided not to. He wanted to play it.

Lance blushed. "So this company bought the rights?"

"They did," Juanita sipped her drink. "We go live next spring. They're actually testing the game right now at all the sex conventions around North America."

"Holy!" Lance said. "Congratulations."

"I couldn't help but notice, Lancey, that you've had a look at one, two, three, four cards," Juanita said, "you have to answer all of them. If you don't, we get to dare you to do whatever we want—and there are two of us."

Lance's eyes widened in complete embarrassment. "Wait. So that's two dares for each one?"

Juanita nodded. "That's if you don't answer or do what the card demands."

"Hold on," Lance said, flustered and aroused all at once. "Easy now. Shari didn't even do hers."

"I know," Juanita said. "And that's why we get to dare her to do two things after we're done."

"Done what?" Lance thought. He realized that this was all a beautiful trap. The whole night had been the perfect web to get them all together. The songs they'd been asked to bring— he knew it was for them to play as they all made love together —or cuddled. He just knew it.

"Darlings," Juanita said. "You two are going to conceive the most beautiful daughter. I've seen her in my dreams. I am carrying her and she's fallen asleep between my breasts. In my dream—that's the most curious thing of all—I still have my breasts. Your little girl—I can never see her face—is carrying little shoes and she's sleeping. You're walking beside me, holding hands. We're by the ocean. I'm positive it's Kits. My heart is singing and we've just come from the most fantastic meal together. We have our whole lives ahead of us raising your little girl and I'm the crazy auntie. I'll always be her favourite."

Lance listened and realized that both he and Shari were wiping the tears away from their eyes. Juanita continued and looked at them both. "I'm going to survive this. I know it. My dreams show me this and I believe them."

"Amen," Shari said softly. "Yes."

"And I want to know which card you put back, Darling, and, Lancey, which cards you've just read," Juanita said, and they all started laughing.

Where will I kiss you next? Lance thought. *What's a little desire between friends?* "Wait," he said. "What's the time limit for any of these?"

"Here's the magic," Juanita said and leaned forward. "They're up when one of you says they're up."

"You sexual goddess," Shari said as she rose to hug Juanita. They embraced and were laugh-crying. "Thank you for telling us about your dream. It's beautiful."

"What's beautiful," she said, "is what I'm about to dare you to do." She looked at Lance. "Lancey, do you have a dare for your wife?"

"Oh yes, Lancey," Shari said. "You know I never back down."

That was true: he had married a warrior woman who loved a challenge.

Lance realized that he had a goofy grin on his face. He beamed. The night was still young. They were hot from the beach, fed on a supper they'd prepared together. They were under Juanita's star blanket and he wasn't necessarily sure he wanted to this to end.

He realized that he still had all four cards in his hand. The letters DARE caught the candlelight.

"Lance," Juanita looked at him coolly. "Do you want to play?"

"Diplomatic immunity," Shari said and hugged Juanita gently.

"Oh, Sister," Juanita started laughing. "After I'm done daring you what I've always wanted to, there won't be any immunity for anyone."

Lance shivered. He felt the eyes of the two women he loved most in the world watching him.

DARE.

He felt the hottest blood inside of him bloom under his skin.

He looked at all four of the cards in his hands.

And then he turned them over.

The Rock Beat

"Up yours, Mister Russell!"

He threw one of my cigarettes over his shoulder. "What?"

"You frickin' told me that my kinda smokes would give me a hairy bum, and I trusted you, and I gave you my pack and now you're smoking them, and I'm stuck with your Big Chief smokes and it's all just frickin' B.S!"

"What are you talking about?"

"You frickin' lied to me. You're smoking my smokes."

"Clarence, it's too late for me. Who cares if I have a hairy ass? I'm lookin' out for you."

"*Wha! As if.*"

"Look: what is it?"

"What do you mean?"

"You can't blame this all on me."

"What are you talking about?"

"Why are you so upset? What's on your mind? Just spit it out. I can tell."

I didn't want to ugly-cry but it I couldn't stop it. "Well, it's frickin' B.S. You know. You always say that if we know the rock beat that you'll let us play for the whole frickin' Band class, and I frickin' practise. Like, my dad used to be a drummer and he showed me, and I frickin' show him every night, and he's like, 'That's the frickin' rock beat.' And I show it to you and you keep picking the triplets and all the hot girls, and I think you just like watching their jugs bounce when they frickin' play."

"Okay. Did you just say 'Jugs!?'" He was trying not to laugh. "That's—that's it? That's all you got? That's the only thing that's upsetting you?"

"Yeah, and another thing is, like, we can tell that you party all weekend. Like you got the frickin' good guitars and frickin' really deadly primo drum kit that no one's allowed to touch, and all we frickin' do is sing and we never get to frickin' play. Like we frickin' sing stuff from the '80s, like "Come on, Eileen" and "Africa" by Toto and you type out the lyrics and you don't even know that the lyrics say that it's Serengeti."

"What?"

"You put dash-dash-dash-question mark 'cause you don't know what he's saying. It's frickin' Serengeti. Even my mom knew that."

"It's Serengeti?"

"Yeah."

"Take it easy. You know I've listen to that Toto song thirty years now and I thought it was Ferengeti."

"Well, it's Serengeti."

"Hunh. Go figure. So that's it? That's all you got."

I wiped my eyes. "Yeah."

"Look, man. I been married twice. I'm payin' alimony, and I saw you with your smokes that I've always wanted to try and, okay, maybe they don't give you a hairy bum—but they could, you know. Do you really want a hairy ass your whole life?"

"No."

"Well, there you go. So you're telling me you got the rock beat?"

"Yeah. I had the rock beat for three years."

"Well, then show me, baby. Let's see what you got."

"Are you serious?"

"Yeah. If you can frickin' nail it, I'll give you an A plus, and you can do the rock beat on Monday."

"Are you really being serious?"

"Yeah, let's see what you got, baby!"

Boom Boom Tsh. Boom Boom Tsh. Boom Boom Tsh.

So I started doing it. I started doing the rock beat. I frickin' nailed it, man. I frickin' nailed it. I been practising in my jammies, my gonchies and my long johns. I did the rock beat until I became the rock beat. Next thing I knew Mr. Russell was doing the rock beat with me, and we were swaying and smiling and he was grinning and he's, like, "Frick, man. Frick. You got it, Clarence. You got it!"

I'm like, "Yeah, I frickin' got it. I had it for years."

He goes, "Yeah, you said it. There you go."

Wheetago War

We are the new Dene. I see this every day. I was born after the twinning of the sun and in the haunted way of the Dog People. I was born running. We are all born hunted now. I sometimes wake up a girl; I sometimes wake up a boy. I don't question this anymore. I just am.

I always go to the water to help out. I am not yet adult but no longer a child. They call me Water Boy but this is a trick. I was blessed in the Water Way so I watch the shores with those of my order. When I'm older I will fight. For now I lead water runs from the waterfall. You don't waste water when you have to haul your own. I am proud of this. Our camp is very respectful and the water returns her favour Her way.

This one time I found boys crucifying a bullfrog. The biggest I've ever seen. It had the legs and chest of a child. I beat those boys and told them I'd report them later to Yellow Hand.

I took that frog and bathed him. I begged him to think of his family, how they missed him, how they must have been wondering where he was.

"Think of your mom," I said. "Your dad must be weeping for you."

He was weak. He kept rolling sideways but I helped him. I sang the spider song to him.

"Nah nah na na nan nah nah
Nah nah nah nah nah
Na na nah nah nah
Weet
weet
weet."

I went into the water and we found shade under the second sun, the one to the left.

We sat and I rocked him. I ran my hands over his belly. He was like a human that way: a baby. I prayed.

I said, "Mother, if you are still here—and there are people in camp who say no—but if you are here and you save him I will believe in you again. I promise."

That is when the frog spoke to me. He whispered. I heard him. He said, "My girl, because you saved me, because you prayed with me and waited for my strength to return, I will give you my medicine."

I grew quiet but not scared. I've learned to move through anything that grabs me with fear.

I said, "Oh... what can you do with your inkwo?"

The frog said I could travel in dreams. I could heal with my hands. I could do so many things.

But then I asked him the question Iris taught us all to ask when we are visited. I said, "But what is the cost?"

"Oh now," he said, "well, if you have our medicine, you can't do this. And when you are on your time, you mustn't do that." This list was too long to remember in one sitting.

I said, "It is like those with bear medicine. They can't be around cats. They get sick fast when cats are near."

He said, "Yes, it is like that."

I said no. "I thank you but I want to have children one day. Those who have your medicine must never have children."

He said there were three in the world who did.

It made me happy to know there were other camps left in the world where medicine was being passed, but I said no.

He looked at me for a while and said, "You have to let me save your life once. I can see what's coming for you."

I said "Okay. Just once. But I don't want your medicine."

He agreed and he asked me to stay with him for a while before his people came.

"Are you a boy or a girl?" he asked.

"I don't know," I said. "I think I am both."

He reached out to touch my face and I let him.

I wish I could say I remember what we spoke about. I think we sang. I think he told me that we could have stopped this, that the Wheetago have always counted on our greed—even from under the ice: our digging, the Rape of our Great Mother, to call them back.

Soon there was rustling in the weeds around us and then a song that rippled the water so gently from other frogs. It was their breath. Together. Around us.

He sang back and then he left.

"I won't forget you," he said.

"I won't forget you," I said.

Then, now, I left and did not tell anyone what happened. I did not tell Yellow Hand or Iris, but those boys always brought me blackberries after.

That was their way of saying sorry.

One almost-summer later, I felt a hood swoop over me as I was getting water and I was lifted by the Wheetago. I knew it was them because of their ankles clicking as they ran. They are like the caribou that way.

I thought *this is it: my time is now.* Take me fast, I said to the Great Wonder. Take me quick.

They knew to move through the willows in a way so they did not slap each other as they passed. I could hear birds above me. The feather of their wings. But I did not hear them. No breath. I named these ones *the shadowless.* The Wheetago bite and somehow decide who gets to turn like them and there are those they torture, decorate and eat. I did not want to be sewn into the trees like some of the children we'd found. Why was I being stolen away?

I prayed hard. I prayed quiet. I prayed to our Mother and to the memory of the Dog People to remember me when my time came. I don't know how long the Wheetago had me but they stopped suddenly, stood me up and pulled my hood off.

I looked down but saw quick with my eyes.

These were not Hair Eaters, who always travel in threes. These were not their Shark Mouths whose jaws drag through the earth or the Almost Birthers who are born suffering worse than the others. These were not the hooked beaked or the ones who can soar off the earth now or hover or dive over water. These had webs and sticks pushed through their skin. These were not six. These were nine.

They had guards facing away from me, much like we do. All three sniffed the air and looked left to right. What was it they feared? I wondered. It was as if they were being chased, too.

I heard the great wet and chewing chambers in their throat and chests surge within them as the six around me argued. It must have been agony not to rip me apart. One grabbed my jaw and I looked at their clawed feet. They were giants. Bigger than men. The rotting rolled off of them like neck meat gone bad. They examined me and I shifted from boy to girl, girl to boy. The only constant was the dog constellation marking my face. I call it the focus. I've watched myself bloom back and forth and it's the only part of me that stays.

The lead bull grabbed my chin hard and made me face him. I saw nothing but hate in its eyes. He had tusks. What was once human looked like it had found a sharp rock and slammed its face first over and over to break its teeth into shards and its mouth into a hole. One eye was open. The other was torn and leaking. One carried a bag sewn into its chest I had seen on a woman when I was a child. She used to nurse the orphans. And I smelled mint. She used it to call her milk. She nursed me when I was abandoned for what I was and how I shifted.

I started to cry.

The lead bull made me look at it, and it used sign language to speak to me. I saw light under its nails. The one to his left—a female—watched me. Another made clicks to the guards and one returned a low growl back. They were talking. We knew they prayed together, but this was the first time I ever heard talk between them.

The lead bull made me know that something spoke to all of them. It pointed to all their eyes. I saw that they had tusks: on their heads and under their chins like the shovels of caribou. This voice warned them. It pointed at me and then it pointed to the earth. It pointed to the sky. It pointed to where I'd come from. The others then stood behind in line and I realized more Wheetago were coming. The trees swayed as they made their way through the forest. They did this so I could not see their numbers. I felt how tall and cold they were behind me. I was nothing to them.

The third to his right then knelt and drew in the sand with its hooked claw how to go home. I'll never forget this: each finger had two claws. One that retracted, the other like a talon.

The lead bull pushed me and I ran. I ran all the way home. The distance that took them minutes to steal took me two hours to run back.

I was going to tell Iris and Old Man but they were gone when I came back. That was their way. Always in ceremony. I say this now to all of you: I know it was that frog. He saved me. I pray he saves me always. This is an animal war, too.

We are a world at war with the Wheetago and Mary, their mother, he told me. She gives birth to all of them through her mouth, they say. But there are those who don't listen to her now: new scouts, new raiding parties, the ones who sew inside-out bodies into the trees.

I know he told me this.

The new scouts carry trophies of their kills. Fetuses. Noses. The wet of us in pieces.

It's as if they're trying to remember something.

They are still hollowing out the earth. Reaching places men in their greed couldn't. There are mountains in the sky now of bones and rock. Altars, maybe.

It's as if they want the world to warm.

Our scouts say that they pray with the rotation of the moon and that the sun twinning was part of something older than the world. Something ancient and starving.

They were always here. Dreaming under ice.

They were the ones who lit the world on fire to bring the ash rain, the red lighting, the shedding of the sun. Even the oceans burned until the fish peeled from their skins because of them.

The Wheetago had years to plan this under the ice of the world. They scared the moon away. They are wishing for something that is not us. They have their gods, too, but we are in their way now.

So the animals and us, we have our medicine back now because the earth, she does not want this. She is wounded and scared and bleeding and we have to help Her. All of us.

This is the rape of her in a new way and she's asking us for help.

She wants to live. They want to take her power. They want to turn the world and everyone here who is not them. So I will fight.

I have to.

I want my children—if I can have them—to know that I chose the muktuk when I was at the Choosing. They say I pulled myself past the caribou meat.

This is why I guard the water. This is why I've marked myself in the way of the Dog Soldier. I will fight for what we have found as a people, and I will help our Mother. I have to.

I have sat with Old Man and his fox and helped him with the Choosing Ceremony. I have used my mother's ulu to prepare the muktuk. This one time when we were done we looked west under the Twin Suns. We saw woman laughing, cooking together. We saw men hauling water and preparing dry fish, dry meat. Children were running, playing. Boys were off to check the nets. Women of all nations were tanning moose hides. "What a shame," he said sadly, "that it took the Wheetago War to make what's left of us finally work together as one people, the new Dene."

He wiped the back of his hands over his eyes. He had been weeping. He took his cane and walked to where his wife would be waiting. He seemed so sad.

Fox followed them to where they lived. They call that fox his little brother, but I have heard him call his friend, "Grandpa."

One time Old Man gave me three small feathers and asked me to bead them in a way so they would always be together. They were so beautiful. I had seen them before in a woman's hair. I forget her name. It must be his symbol for hope, family, grace. They smelled of yarrow, sweet grass, the wick of buffalo sage. I sewed them together in her memory and in the memory of the family we've had to become. When I gave them back to him, he smiled. He rolled that bullet of his in his hand and I saw smoke rolling off his palm. Not smoke from fire, but smoke from ice. His hands were covered in burns: open and old. "Mahsi, my girl," he said.

Fox looked at him with his torn and folded ear. He smiled, too. Still, I am curious. Those guards that surrounded us. The way they sniffed the air. They were being tracked. By what, I don't know. The new breed of them changes all the time. Perhaps they are hunting each other. This would bring hope if it were true.

My true name is Dove. I am both a boy and a girl and I don't question anything anymore. I want to live. We all, including our Great Mother, want to live.

I don't care that a north wind will blow now that I've told you about them.

Let's fight.

A ho.

Tapwe.

Dawe.

Prayers

For those taken
Too soon
By those they loved
and trusted...

Afterwords

Mahsi cho for reading my stories. I would like to dedicate the spirit of this collection to the memory of Dr. Renate Eigenbrod. As well, I would like to thank Janine Cheeseman and Tracy Essex-Simpson at Aurora Artists for their incredible representation. I would also like to acknowledge the support of the MacEwan University Writer in Residence program, where I was proud to serve as their Writer in Residence in 2013 and 2014 and hone this collection. Maurice Mierau and Catharina de Bakker, mahsi cho for editing all of my stories with Enfield & Wizenty. I am grateful.

"bornagirl" is dedicated to Annelies Pool.

"Where are you tonight?" is dedicated to Anita Doron, Christina Piovesan, Alex Lalonde, Joel Evans, Kiowa Gordon, Adam Butcher, Chloe Rose, Benjamin Bratt, Tony Rabesca and everyone who had anything to do with the making of *The Lesser Blessed*, the movie, with First Generation Films. Mahsi cho!!

"The Strongest Blood" is dedicated to Earl, Marlene, Trevor and Ty Evans

"I Double Dogrib Dare You" is dedicated to Joel Duthie, Casey Germain and Graeme Comyn.

"Blood Rides the Wind" is dedicated to Garry Gottfriedson because he inspires me in all the right ways. I've always wanted to write one of those Continuum 33 1/3 books where an author gets to write a whole book inspired by an album. I love Kate Schatz's take on PJ Harvey's *Rid of Me*. "Blood Rides the Wind" is dedicated to Leif Gregersen, Alex Russo and Shane Turgeon. This story is Bear's part two of "The Contract" in *Godless but Loyal to Heaven* with hints of more in "Love Walked In" in *The Moon of Letting Go*. The album that I hear as the backdrop of Bear's narrative in all of his stories (including "The Fleshing" in *Godless but Loyal to Heaven*) is "Disintegration" by The Cure. This album changed my life forever.

"Skull.Full.Of.Rust" is dedicated to the memory of JCS.

"Because of What I Did" is dedicated to Ric and Rose Richardson and Louise Halfe.

"Crow" is dedicated to Chrystos, Katrina Chappell and Gregory Scofield.

"If Only Tonight" is dedicated to everyone you thought of when you read it(!)

"The Rock Beat" is dedicated to my brothers: Roger Wah-shee, Johnny Van Camp and Jamie Van Camp.

"Wheetago War" is dedicated to Antonio Fuso and Art Napoleon.

Thank you for reading my stories. I am grateful to you. Mahsi cho!

Acknowledgements

"The Strongest Blood" *Decolonization: Indigeneity, Education & Society*, Vol. 3, No. 3, University of Alberta Press, 2014.

"Where are you tonight?" *Prairie Fire*, Vol. 34, No. 1, 2013.

"bornagirl" *Coming Home: Stories from The Northwest Territories*, Enfield & Wizenty, 2012.

"Skull.Full.Of. Rust" *mitêwâcimowina: Indigenous Science Fiction and Speculative Storytelling*, Theytus Books, 2015.

An excerpt from "Because of What I Did" is published in *Kwe: Standing With Our Sisters, Penguin Books, 2015.*